THE FAMOUS FIVE AND THE SECRET OF THE CAVES

THE FAMOUS FIVE are Julian, Dick, George (Georgina by rights), Anne and Timmy the dog.

On holiday in Wales, the Five are fascinated by a local tale about the Dark Folk who once lived in the hidden valley of Mount Graig. Curious to discover if there's any truth behind the legend, the Five decide to investigate. But it's not long before they realise that they are not alone in their search for the lost valley and its ancient treasure . . .

Cover illustration by Doug Post.

**Also by the same author,
and available in Knight Books:**

The Famous Five and the Stately Homes
Gang

The Famous Five and the Mystery of the
Emeralds

The Famous Five and the Missing Cheetah

The Famous Five Go On Television

The Famous Five and the Golden Galleon

The Famous Five Versus the Black Mask

The Famous Five and the Blue Bear
Mystery

The Famous Five In Fancy Dress

The Famous Five and the Inca God

The Famous Five and the Cavalier's
Treasure

The Famous Five and the Strange Legacy

The Famous Five and the Secret of the Caves

A new adventure of the characters created by Enid Blyton, told by Claude Voilier, translated by Anthea Bell

Illustrated by Bob Harvey

KNIGHT BOOKS
Hodder and Stoughton

Copyright © Librairie Hachette 1976

First published in France as *Les Cinq dans la Cité Secrète*

English language translation copyright © Hodder & Stoughton
Ltd, 1984
Illustrations copyright © Hodder & Stoughton Ltd, 1984

First published in Great Britain by Knight Books 1984
Second impression 1985

British Library C.I.P.

Voilier, Claude
    The Famous Five and the secret of the caves.
    I. Title   II. Les Cinq dans la cité secrète.
    English
    843'.914[J]   PZ7

ISBN 0-340-35336-8

Printed and bound in Great Britain for
Hodder and Stoughton Paperbacks, a
division of Hodder and Stoughton Ltd.,
Mill Road, Dunton Green, Sevenoaks,
Kent (Editorial Office: 47 Bedford
Square, London, WC1 3DP) by
Hunt Barnard Printing Ltd,
Aylesbury, Bucks.

CONTENTS

Philip Mackintosh
P5 44 Grigor Driv
IV2 4LS

Chapter One

BACK TO MAGGA GLEN FARM

'Honestly, George,' said Julian, 'I'm *sure* we'll enjoy our holidays here in Wales just as much as if we'd stayed in Kirrin the whole time! Don't you remember what fun we had in Magga Glen before?'

George Kirrin looked at her cousin with a very discontented expression on her face. She had been born and lived all her life by the seaside, and she loved swimming and taking her rowing boat out on the sea, so she hadn't been a bit pleased when her parents told her they were all going to spend three or four weeks in Magga Glen, a village high up in the Welsh mountains.' 'All' included George's cousins Julian, Dick and Anne, who had come to spend the summer holidays with her as usual. Aunt Fanny and Uncle Quentin were always pleased to have their nephews and niece to stay.

Yes, George did remember the couple of weeks

they had spent at old Mrs Jones's farmhouse when they were all getting better from the 'flu – and she remembered the exciting adventure they had had, too! All the same, she wasn't going to let Julian win her over so easily.

'That's all very well,' she grumbled, 'but there isn't going to be anything to *do*! It was winter when we came to Magga Glen farm last time, and we could toboggan and play in the snow. You can't do any of that in summer – and either the weather's too hot for comfort, or it's so chilly you have to wear layers of woollies! Oh, I wish we hadn't had to come here!'

'Do cheer up, George!' said Anne in her soft voice. 'There'll be lots to do – I'm sure there will!'

But George still didn't seem convinced. She was just eleven, with curly dark hair which she kept short like a boy's. Her bright eyes and quick movements showed how full of energy she was. Her younger cousin Anne was very different. *She* had pretty, fair hair and blue eyes, and she was a gentle little girl who hardly ever said a cross word.

Julian, who was thirteen, was the eldest of the four cousins. He smiled at his little sister. He was fair-haired, like Anne, and tall for his age – and he was the most sensible and responsible of all four children.

'Of course there'll be lots to do!' he said enthusiastically. 'Just as much as there is to do at Kirrin Cottage, I bet!'

Kirrin Cottage was George's home – it was near

Kirrin village, and her very own island, Kirrin Island, stood out in the sea opposite the house. It isn't every little girl who actually owns an island, so perhaps it wasn't very surprising that George was reluctant to come away to Wales.

Dick agreed with his brother, however, and he nodded his head. He was the same age as George, and since he was dark too they looked rather alike. All the more so because George liked to act as if she were a boy herself – she often wished she *had* been born a boy instead of a girl!

'Julian's right!' said Dick firmly. 'And what *really* matters is for the Five to be together for the holidays, isn't it?'

George suddenly cheered up when he reminded her of this. It certainly *was* the most important thing! The Five consisted of the four children and George's dog Timothy – Timmy or Tim for short. She and dear old Timmy were inseparable companions. George turned to her dog.

'Well, what do *you* say, Timmy?' she asked him.

'Woof!' replied Timmy, wagging his tail.

'There you are!' said Dick, laughing. 'He's perfectly happy here, now he's made friends with Morgan's sheepdogs!' Morgan was the farmer, and Mrs Jones was his mother – when the children came to Magga Glen before, Timmy and the sheepdogs didn't get on at all well at first, but the eight dogs had been very brave tackling some bad men who were mining precious metal and smuggling it out to sea down an underground river, and after that they were firm friends!

'I bet you anything Timmy expects us to have another adventure, just as exciting as the one we had here in the winter!' Dick added. 'Adventures do seem to come our way – and he knows it!'

'Well, adventure or no adventure – and an adventure isn't actually *guaranteed*, you know!' said Julian, sensibly, 'I think we'd better decide how else we're going to spend our time.'

They had arrived only the day before, and they hadn't had time to explore and see what the mountains were like in summertime yet. The reason why they had all come to Wales was that Uncle Quentin had been overworking, and the doctor said he had to have a complete rest – a holiday away from home, so that he wouldn't be tempted to shut himself up in his study and go on with his important scientific research. Aunt Fanny immediately thought of Magga Glen Farm. She knew that old Mrs Jones let rooms in the farmhouse to holiday-makers, because the children had been there once already, on their own. Magga Glen was such a quiet, peaceful place that she felt sure it would do Uncle Quentin good – and very luckily, Mrs Jones was able to have them just when they wanted to go!

'Now, children,' Aunt Fanny had told George and her cousins when they arrived, 'I know you'll be able to amuse yourselves. I want to spend as much time as I can with your father, George – he's supposed to sit in the sun and rest, or go for nice gentle walks, and if I'm not there to keep an eye on him I'm sure he'll be burying himself in books again, which is just what the doctor did *not* order!'

The children laughed – they knew that Uncle Quentin had insisted on bringing a heavy suitcase full to the brim with books and papers!

'So I leave it to you to do whatever you like,' Aunt Fanny went on. 'All I ask is that you'll be on time for meals, so as not to put kind Mrs Jones to any trouble, and not do anything silly!'

'As if we would!' said George, indignantly.

'Hm!' replied her father. Obviously he didn't quite trust her! 'Julian, I want you to look after the others, please – don't forget you're the eldest. I know I can trust *you*!'

Julian took his position as the eldest very seriously, as Uncle Quentin realised. Anne never gave her big brother any trouble – but George could be very impulsive, and Dick was inclined to be mischievous, so he often had his work cut out with them!

All the children thought Julian's suggestion was a good one. They went out to sit in Mrs Jones's pretty little garden, which had a stone wall to shelter it from the mountain winds, and drew up plans for their holiday in Wales. Julian took a bus timetable out of his pocket.

'There are plenty of buses and coaches,' he told the others. 'So we can have some good expeditions to interesting places in Wales – and if we don't want to go quite so far, well, we've brought our bicycles with us! We can explore the countryside by bike, or walk if the hills are too steep for much cycling.'

'I've got an idea we'll be doing quite a *lot* of walking!' said George. 'There are steep hills and mountains *everywhere* here, and that means hard work cycling up them!'

'But it means an easy ride going down too!' Dick pointed out.

'Anyway, Magga Glen Farm makes a very good starting point for our excursions,' said Julian.

'Yes – and Mrs Jones is a very good cook, too!' said Dick happily. He was remembering all the delicious things to eat Mrs Jones cooked them when they came to Wales before. There was a dreamy look in his eyes!

'Dick, you're thinking of her apple pie!' George said. All the cousins knew that if Dick wasn't exactly *greedy* – still, he did like his food!

The children all laughed. They stood up, brushed the bits of grass and leaves off their clothes, and decided that the first thing they'd do after dinner would be to go into Magga Glen village itself. They hadn't seen very much of it when they were staying with Mrs Jones before, because they had spent most of their time skiing in the mountains above the farmhouse.

Dinner was quite up to Dick's expectations – and it *did* finish with apple pie! They set off on their bicycles straight afterwards. Timmy was delighted to have a chance to stretch his legs, and he ran along beside George, chasing off the road now and then to investigate the moorland beside it.

'He misses the Kirrin rabbits, so he's looking for *Welsh* rarebits!' said Dick, and everyone laughed at this terrible joke.

It was downhill nearly all the way to the village. Magga Glen was a pretty little place, with a church, a number of low-built white cottages with grey slate roofs, and one or two shops. It was surrounded by rolling green hills, but when you looked up you saw the moors and the mountains beyond. The Five walked round the village for a bit, and then decided they were feeling thirsty. There was one little teashop in the place, with some chairs and tables outside it, and as it was a fine day the children went to sit at one of the tables.

'Let's see if we can buy some lemonade!' suggested George.

Timmy lay down under the table beside her. Quite soon a young waitress came out of the teashop, smiling at the children. 'Hallo!' she said, with a pretty, soft Welsh accent. 'And what can I do for you, bach?' she asked Julian, as the eldest.

The children knew, from their earlier visit to Wales, that 'bach' meant 'dear'. Julian ordered the lemonade, and a bowl of water for Timmy, whose tongue was hanging out! The waitress said they had Welsh cakes, too, freshly baked on an iron griddle – that was like a flat, heavy frying pan, she explained, and the cakes were cooked on it on top of the stove. The children ordered some of those too, and when they came they were delicious, with lots of currants and spice in them.

The friendly waitress stopped to chat with them for a few minutes. 'Is it your first visit to Wales, then?' she asked.

'No, we've been to Magga Glen before,' George explained. 'We stayed at Magga Glen Farm, where we're staying now, but it was winter, so we didn't get about to explore the countryside much. Is there anything interesting to go and see near here?'

'Well now, that's not easy to say, bach,' said the waitress. 'There's plenty of pretty walks to take – and if it's legends and old stories you like, we've plenty of them too!' she added, smiling.

'Oh, I love legends and stories!' said Anne.

'Why then, it's the legend of Mount Graig you'll be liking to hear!' said the girl.

'Tell it to us – please do!' Anne begged, but just then some more customers came and sat down at the next table, and the waitress shook her head.

'I've my work to do, bach, now haven't I?'

But seeing Anne's imploring gaze, she thought for a moment, and then said, 'I'll tell you what now! Just you go and see old Branwen! She knows all the local stories, old Branwen does – she's the oldest woman in the village, indeed she is, and glad she'd be to see your young faces, and have someone new to hear her tales. Tell her it was Dilys sent you, bach!'

And Dilys told the children where old Branwen lived, before she hurried off to take her new

customers' order.

The four cousins finished their lemonade and Welsh cakes, paid the bill, got on their bicycles, and cycled off down the village street. Branwen lived at the very end of it – and by now they were feeling really intrigued! They could hardly wait to hear the legend of Mount Graig!

Chapter Two

THE LEGEND OF MOUNT GRAIG

The children found Branwen sitting outside her cottage door in the sun, warming her rheumaticky fingers, with her hands clasped over the knob of a big stick. She certainly did seem to be a very old lady, but she smiled as if she was pleased to see them. Julian very politely explained why they had come, and old Branwen smiled at them again.

'Well now, it's pleased I am to have young visitors!' she told them. 'So it's the legend of Mount Graig you wanted to hear? Gather round, my dears, and I'll tell you the story . . .'

George and Anne sat down on the seat outside the old lady's door with her, and the boys sat on the low stone wall opposite.

'Once upon a time –' old Branwen began, and George had to do her best not to look disappointed! She was afraid that Branwen was going to tell them some ordinary fairy tale that they knew perfectly well already.

17

But she was wrong! A few moments later her eyes were shining as she listened to the old woman's story, intent upon every word of it. For it really was a fascinating tale.

A very strange legend, Branwen told her young hearers, had grown up around the mountain, in the village of Graig at its foot, and had been handed down over the centuries. She explained that 'Graig' just meant 'crag', and the mountain took its name from its rocky, crag-like appearance. 'It's the mountain you can see over there,' she said. And she pointed to the peak which topped a gently rolling slope. It was next to the mountainside where Magga Glen farmhouse itself stood.

'Yes, and the village has the same name, Graig,' she went on. 'Now, my dears, believe it or not, but the villagers have always claimed that their mountain is hollow!'

'Hollow?' repeated Anne in surprise. 'But if it was true, then it wouldn't be a very *strong* mountain, would it? You might step right through if you tried climbing it!'

The old woman smiled.

'That depends!' she said. 'If you had enough of the thickness of the earth's crust between you, bach, then you'd not be stepping through! But indeed, they don't mean it's *all* hollow inside, but there's holes, you see, caves and tunnels – like one of those queer foreign cheeses full of holes!'

The children couldn't help smiling at this comparison, but they understood what Branwen

18

meant.

'Although they do say there's a real hollow in the middle of the mountain,' she went on. 'Yes, they say there's a lost valley there, where folk once lived who came from some far place, no one knows where, and those folk were swept away as if they'd never been, by some disaster – yes, indeed!'

Branwen stopped, as if to see what effect her story was having on her hearers. Julian was listening politely, but he showed only a slight interest in it. He was too down-to-earth to believe in such a fantastic tale!

Anne, however, was listening entranced. She didn't *really* believe Branwen's story was true, in her heart, but she would have *liked* to believe it! Anne was very fond of fairy tales, and in everyday life she was a bit inclined to go in for daydreaming.

Dick was rather more interested in watching his cousin's reactions than in the story itself. George's face, as *she* listened, was a real picture! Her eyes and her expression showed everything she was thinking as she heard the legend of Mount Graig. You could read her like a book, thought Dick. She was thinking that there's a little kernel of truth in every legend, and that it would be interesting to try disentangling the true part of this particular story from the invented bits!

'Do *you* believe the legend yourself?' she asked the old woman abruptly.

Branwen was taken by surprise. She thought for a moment and then shook her head. 'Dear me, bach, *I* don't know!' she said. 'I dare say it's mostly lies, indeed!'

'Yes, that's just what I was thinking,' said George.

'Although it could be true,' the old lady went on, 'that there were folk who had to take refuge inside the mountain . . .'

'Always supposing it really *is* hollow!' Dick pointed out.

'It may be, bach, it may be!' said Branwen. 'There might have been a valley, to be sure – perhaps there still is!'

'Well, in that case,' said Julian, in a matter-of-fact way, 'how is it that no one's ever found it? I suppose people *have* looked?'

'Oh yes, yes indeed! But then again, bach, perhaps the disaster of the legend blocked the way in, who can tell?'

George was getting more and more interested. She leaned forward. 'Have you got any idea what *kind* of a disaster it was?' she asked. 'Could it have been a seismic disturbance?'

Old Branwen didn't understand.

'A what?' she asked, looking blank.

'Well, like a kind of little earthquake – an earth tremor!'

The old lady looked at her sharply. She seemed both surprised and rather admiring! 'Now what made you think that, bach? For it's just what I believe myself! There *have* been earth tremors in these parts, yes indeed! Quite severe, I once heard, for anywhere in the British Isles! Why, there've been three in Graig village itself in the last hundred and fifty years! But how did you guess?' she insisted. She never took her eyes off George.

George laughed. 'Well, it wasn't very difficult!' she said. 'If the way into this secret valley was hidden by rocks or earth it seems likely to have been as the result of an earth-fall – and it's only when there's an earthquake that that happens so suddenly and dramatically!'

'Gosh, what a brilliant deduction!' said Dick sarcastically. He really admired his cousin, but he wasn't going to admit it in a hurry – he took his chance to tease her whenever he could.

But George was too wrapped up in the story to take any notice of him. As for Julian, *he* was beginning to take a genuine interest in it now.

'Yes,' he said slowly, 'if there have been real earth tremors hereabouts, it does make the story of these people who disappeared sound a bit more likely!'

The four cousins began asking old Branwen lots more questions. They wanted details and dates – but there wasn't much more the old woman could say.

'Oh, dear me, I could have told you once, maybe,' she said sadly. 'But I've been losing my memory these last two years, so I have. And it's a long time since last I told this story, indeed it is! Why don't you go to Graig one of these days, my dears? Try the miller – he's a talkative fellow, he is, and he could likely tell you more. His grandad died last year, and *he* was the best storyteller in this part of Wales!'

The children thanked Branwen very much for her story, and said goodbye. As soon as they got back to Magga Glen Farm they held a consultation. George was full of what they had heard.

'I'm sure the legend has a basis of truth!' she said enthusiastically. 'And as we haven't got an adventure yet, or thought of anything particular to do while we're in Wales, why don't we try to find out what it really *is* based on? It would give a bit of point to our holidays, wouldn't it?'

Dick smiled at his cousin. 'Well, why not?' he said. 'It sounds like the title of an adventure story! The Five and the Lost Valley! Or: The Five on the Trail of the Vanished People!'

'Goodness, George, do you think we could really find out anything?' said Anne.

'Why not?' said George. 'As Dick says! What do *you* think, Ju?'

'Hm – I don't mind *trying*,' said Julian, cautiously. 'But I'd be more inclined to take it as a game! I wouldn't be too hopeful if I were you. After all, George, people like us who felt interested must have been looking for ages. And real experts have probably been trying to discover the secret of Mount Graig, too – archaeologists and anthropologists and so on!'

'But they haven't had any luck!' pointed out Dick. 'Because if they *had* discovered the secret, then it wouldn't be a secret any more, would it?'

'I don't care whether we take it as a game or not, I think it would be *fun*!' said George. 'For one thing, it's a good way to help us explore this part of the country – and for another, we may find useful clues as we do our exploring! Well, do you all agree?'

'All right,' said Julian quietly.

'Oh *yes*!' cried Anne.

Dick just nodded his head vigorously.

'Woof!' said Timmy firmly, not to be left out.

'Right,' said George, in a satisfied tone of voice. 'Then we'll start making our inqui.ies tomorrow – it's too late to begin today. And I think I can hear Mrs Jones calling us!'

Sure enough, old Mrs Jones had come to the kitchen door. She told the children where they would find a patch of wild strawberries on the hillside, and promised them a very special pudding if they brought her enough. The children thought picking wild strawberries was a lovely idea – and eating them, too, although they were very good and didn't eat too many while they picked. It was certainly a good strawberry patch, with plenty of fruit, though picking them was a rather fiddly job.

George picked away, filling her basket with the pretty little red fruits, but her thoughts were a long way off – and she was feeling very excited!

'We'll start our inquiries tomorrow!' she thought to herself. 'Who knows – they may lead to a real adventure, or we may uncover a piece of history that nobody knew about before!'

Before the children went to bed that evening, they went out into the farmhouse garden and looked at Mount Graig. It stood out against the blue night sky, looking very black, against a background of twinkling stars.

'Oh, look at those stars!' said Anne quietly, in a thoughtful voice. 'Perhaps the people of the lost valley once used to gaze at them and dream! Perhaps the stars saw them come here – and saw them go!'

'Ah, if only they could talk!' said Dick, sarcastically, laughing at his sentimental little sister.

'Well, we'll find out more tomorrow, I'm sure,' said George. 'If we go round asking questions, even at random, we're bound to pick up more details of the legend at the very least!'

'But meanwhile let's get some rest,' suggested Julian. 'Come on, bedtime! We'll have quite a long way to cycle tomorrow – and some of it will be uphill!'

Next morning the children got up quite early. They had asked kind Mrs Jones to make them some sandwiches for a picnic, and she had left them big packets of food to take. They expected to spend the whole day over on Mount Graig.

The way there was rather too much for Timmy – and after a couple of kilometres George picked him up and put him in her bicycle basket. He looked grand riding there, like a king in his royal coach!

It was a pleasant ride to Graig, and all the

children were in a good mood when they got there. The village was rather smaller than the village of Magga Glen, and the Five found the miller old Branwen had mentioned quite easily. In fact he was a baker and not really a miller – but he lived in what had once been the mill for grinding flour, and so he was known as 'Dai the Mill' in the village. He had some delicious-looking iced buns in his window, and Julian bought some for the picnic. When he had paid for the buns, he explained what brought them to Graig.

'So it's Branwen sent you, eh?' said Dai, smiling. 'And you're interested in the legend of Mount Graig, are you, then?'

'Oh yes!' George assured him fervently. 'We know the rough outlines of it – but we *would* like to fill in the details!'

'Ah, I'm afraid I've no time to do that, bach, not with the baking and all – but there's my little girl Gwenny, she often used to listen to her great-grandpa's stories! Gwenny!' he called.

A dark-haired little girl of about twelve came into the shop. She and the Five took to each other at once – and George and her cousins were relieved to find that she spoke perfect English! Last time they had been in Wales they had made friends with a little girl called Aily who spoke only Welsh, except for a few words – but while Gwenny had the pretty Welsh accent of all the mountain people hereabouts, she spoke English to the children. She told them that both languages were used at her school, and she and her parents spoke both Welsh and English at home too.

'Off you go and have a talk out of doors,' said Dai the Mill. So many children were rather in his way inside the baker's shop! 'I've work to be done!'

Anne had a good idea. She invited Gwenny to come and share their picnic – then they'd have plenty of time to talk! Gwenny and Dai liked the idea too, and Dai gave the children a present of a loaf of fruit bread, just out of the bakery oven, which he said was called 'bara brith'.

'Come along!' Gwenny told her new friends. 'I know a good picnic place, in the meadow at the foot of the mountain here!'

It *was* a good picnic place – there were birds singing in the sky above them, and they could hear the distant bleating of sheep on the hills as they sat and ate their picnic. What with Mrs Jones's sandwiches, the iced buns and the bara brith, and a little basket of ripe red and yellow gooseberries that Gwenny had brought too, there was plenty for everyone, and it was all delicious.

'Now,' said Dick, sitting back with a sigh of well-fed satisfaction, 'tell us about the mysterious people of the lost valley, Gwenny! Aren't there any books of local history giving information about them?'

'No, I don't think so,' Gwenny told him. 'Great-grandpa used to say the legend had always been passed on orally, from generation to generation.'

'And what were the people of the valley *like*?'

asked George. 'Nobody's told us that yet.'

'Apparently they were very dark,' said Gwenny, 'and so they were known as the Dark Folk. They were said to have rather swarthy skins and black hair, like gypsies.'

'So now we know what they were said to *look* like,' said George. 'But what did they do – how did they live? Were they hunters or farmers, or what?'

Gwenny began to laugh. 'To hear you talk, George, anyone would think they really existed, but you know, that's not at all certain.'

'Still, if the legend says what they looked like it might say how they lived too,' said Dick. That seemed logical!

Gwenny thought for a little while. 'As far as I remember, Great-grandpa said very little was known about them, but of course they did go hunting –'

'Well, they'd have had to, to get food!' said George, a little impatiently. 'We're talking about hundreds and hundreds of years ago, I suppose, when most of this part of the country would have been forest, except for the mountain slopes. There must have been game for them to catch!'

Gwenny looked at Timmy, who was enjoying the very last of the bara brith. Then she smiled at George. 'Your dog Timmy reminds me of one story about the Dark Folk,' she said.

Everyone waited, with bated breath!

'They were said to keep dogs that never barked!' said Gwenny. 'What do you think of *that*, Tim?'

'Woof!' said Timmy, disapprovingly.

The four cousins couldn't make any sense of this. 'Dogs that didn't bark?' said Dick. 'That's ridiculous! *Why* didn't they bark?'

'I don't know,' said Gwenny. 'I'm only telling you what the legend says.'

'But all hunting dogs bark sometimes, when they're chasing game, or to let the huntsmen know when they've found it!'

'Well, perhaps these dogs were different,' said Gwenny.

George was staring into space with a faraway look in her eyes. 'So their dogs didn't bark,' she said. 'All right, it's a peculiar detail, but we can't get much farther on that point. Go on, Gwenny. What else do you know about the Dark Folk?'

'Well, they were led by –'

'A king?' suggested Dick, interested.

'No, a queen! Her name was Zulma.'

'Gosh!' said Dick. 'That sounds more Eastern than Welsh, doesn't it!'

'Shut up, Dick!' snapped George. 'Stop interrupting Gwenny!'

'It might make sense if they *were* part of some kind of gypsy tribe, though,' said Julian thoughtfully. 'Gypsies do have queens sometimes, don't they? And I read in a book that the word "gypsy" really means "Egyptian", but gypsies actually come from India originally, and their Romany language is descended from Hindi.'

'Goodness, what a lot you know!' said Gwenny,

admiringly.

'Never mind what *he* knows, Gwenny – we want to hear what *you* know!' George told her.

'Well – the legend also says that their settlement in the valley, and the valley itself, both had the name of Temulka!'

'Temulka!' repeated Dick. 'I wonder what that meant?'

Gwenny only shook her head.

'Do you know any more?' asked Julian. He was getting really interested in the story now, in spite of his sceptical attitude at first!

'Yes, I do!' said Gwenny, with a mischievous smile. 'I kept the best bit to tell you last! The Dark Folk were said to have the secret of making gold!'

Chapter Three

IN SEARCH OF CAVES

'Making gold!' repeated George, looking very surprised indeed.

'Yes, making gold! Great-grandpa said they used to worship a statue of their queen, made of solid gold, just as if it were a goddess – because Zulma had the power to cure all illnesses.'

The children were hanging on Gwenny's every word now. 'I must say,' remarked Julian, 'this story is getting more and more fascinating – and less and less likely!'

George leaped to her feet and began pacing up and down. To everyone's amusement, Timmy jumped up too and imitated her, turning whenever she did. He looked very comical!

'Don't forget, this is a legend!' George said. 'That means that everything Gwenny's told us isn't necessarily true – and everything isn't necessarily false either. We must try to divide the bits of the story up! Facts one side, fiction the other! But if you want my opinion, I'm sure these Dark People really *did* exist.'

'So am I!' said Anne, who had been drinking in the whole story.

'Is that really all you know, Gwenny?' asked Dick.

'Yes – but I can show you the best way to climb Mount Graig if you want to explore the mountain,' said Gwenny.

'That's a good idea,' agreed George. 'Let's go and scout round a bit!'

The children packed up the remains of their picnic and hid their bicycles behind some bushes. Then they set off.

Gwenny led them along a sheep track which went across the meadow and up the mountainside. It was quite easy to follow, and they walked along talking happily to each other. Now and then Anne picked some of the wild flowers that grew beside the pathway. As for Timmy, he tried to catch dragonflies and went chasing off after any little animals he saw. They all got away from him!

There was not really very much for George and her cousins to see, except the scenery. On their left, the mountainside sloped gently down to the meadows and moorland below, and on their right the slope rose more steeply. Part of it was bare rock, part had grass, nibbled short by the sheep, and scrubby little bushes growing on it.

'That's the slope we want to look at more

closely,' George murmured to her cousins, under her breath. 'If there really is a valley inside the mountain then we ought to be able to spot the way into it somewhere – even if it's crumbled in a fall of earth or been blocked by rocks.'

She spoke quietly because they didn't want Gwenny to know they seriously intended looking for the valley – she might have laughed at them! So all they did was get to know Mount Graig a little better. Once they reached the top they had a splendid view.

'Isn't Wales beautiful?' said Gwenny proudly.

'Yes,' agreed George, but loyal to her home, she added, 'Not as beautiful as Kirrin, though!'

'Woof!' Timmy agreed. He was tired of mountaineering!

'It's about time we went down again,' said Julian, looking at his watch. 'And I don't want to leave our cycles down there unguarded for too long. Somebody might go off with them.'

'There aren't any dishonest people in *these* parts – whatever it's like in this Kirrin place of yours,' said Gwenny, a little offended.

'Maybe not!' said Dick, laughing. 'But if this whole set of Dark Folk got lost, so might our bikes!'

Chatting and laughing, the children climbed down the mountain again, accompanied by Timmy. Altogether, thought the Five, the first day of their exploration had been quite fruitful. They felt marvellously tired and full of fresh air that evening, and they very quickly dropped off to sleep when they went to bed in their two little bedrooms off the stone passage upstairs in Magga Glen farmhouse.

Next day the Five went out into the garden of the farmhouse to take stock of yesterday's expedition.

'Gwenny was a lot of help,' said George. 'But from what she said, I should think there must be other places where we could get information too.'

Julian looked doubtful. 'I don't agree,' he said. 'Who else could we ask?'

'Yes,' said Dick. 'I don't really see where else we could go!'

'To the schoolteacher!' said George. 'The teacher in the Graig village school. He must know something about the local history of the place, I'm sure!'

'There isn't a school in Graig!' Anne reminded her cousin gently. 'Don't you remember? Gwenny told us she had to go to school in Magga Glen – she's just finished at the junior school there, and now she'll have to take a bus to her new school in town every day!'

'Good!' said George. 'That means we won't have so far to go – and I'm sure the teacher in Magga Glen will be able to answer our questions.'

'There's one thing you're forgetting,' Dick pointed out. 'It's the holidays! I bet you anything the teacher's gone away to have *his* holiday somewhere else. He probably gets bored living in the mountains here and goes to London, or somewhere busy like that, just for a change!'

'Bother! I didn't think of that,' said George. 'Oh well – it's worth trying, anyway! Let's go and ring his doorbell.'

The Five set off at once. When they reached Magga Glen they easily found the school. It was quite a new building – and they were lucky enough to find Mr Williams the teacher at home in his house next to it. He was very friendly, and never guessed that the children were anything but young tourists who wanted some information about local history.

'However, there's really very little I can tell you about the legend,' he said. 'You seem to know the main points already: the dogs that never barked, the fact that these mysterious people were dark-skinned and were said to have the secret of making gold, the healing powers of their queen, Zulma. In fact there's only one more thing I can add: the name Temulka that the Dark Folk are supposed to have given to their settlement in the valley inside the mountain was said to have meant "roaring water".'

'Temulka – roaring water!' Julian repeated slowly.

'Yes, and that rather suggests that there was a river with a fast current flowing through the lost valley – at least, I can't see any other explanation for it.'

George and her cousins thanked Mr Williams, and found themselves out in the village street again, not much wiser than before.

'And there's not much chance that we *will* learn any more just by asking,' said Dick. 'I vote we *do* something – take action! I think it's time to start looking for the way into that secret valley!'

'Just what I was going to suggest myself!' said George. 'Come on, let's go straight back to Graig!'

But Julian reminded her that there were several things they ought to do first – let Aunt Fanny and Uncle Quentin know they were off for the rest of the day, get their climbing shoes, and ask Mrs Jones to pack them up another picnic. Sometimes George forgot these little practical details in her hurry to get things moving as fast as possible.

Less than an hour later, however, the children were cycling cheerfully off to Graig, with Timmy enthroned in his basket. His ears were streaming in the wind as they all rode along.

As soon as the Five reached 'their' meadow they had their picnic – it was mid-day, and they were feeling very hungry. Mrs Jones had given them pork pies and hard-boiled eggs and tomatoes today, as a change from sandwiches, and there were bananas and apples and a delicious moist ginger cake too. Once they had finished, and had packed up the picnic things, they hid their bicycles in the bushes again and began climbing the sheep track which led them up the mountainside.

This time they weren't taking any interest in the flowers or the butterflies or the view. They were all concentrating on examining the steeper, rocky slope of the mountain to their right.

They had gone about five hundred yards up the slope when Dick suddenly stopped to look at a big clump of very tall bracken. The plants seemed to have been crushed by a large animal of some kind – or perhaps a human being – that had plunged through the clump.

'Perhaps it was a sheep?' Anne suggested.

'More likely a man,' said George. 'A sheep would probably have done more damage. I can't say whoever walked through this bracken took *many* precautions – but at least they didn't tread the whole lot down. I wonder if it's hiding anything?'

As George spoke, she parted the tall bracken in front of her and looked behind it. Then she let out a cry of delight.

'I say! There's a cave in here!'

'Come on – let's explore!' said Dick enthusiastically.

The children were properly dressed for this sort of expedition, with good tough jeans and climbing shoes on. That was a good thing, because they had to squeeze through a rather narrow, rough gap in the rocks to get into the cave.

'Maybe this is the way into the lost valley!' said Anne hopefully.

'That's not very likely, Anne,' Julian told her. 'It wouldn't be at all difficult to find this entrance – other people would have been sure to get here before us.'

'And someone, or something, *has* been here be-

fore us, judging by that bracken,' added Dick.

'What's more, they can't have got far!' said George, sounding disappointed. 'As far as I can see this is a tiny little cave which simply comes to a dead end. Still, we must make sure.'

She switched on her torch. Its beam lit up the walls of the cave – sure enough, there was nothing at all mysterious about them! Julian and Dick looked all round the cave for a secret passage, and even felt the rock of the walls, but they didn't find anything at all. The cave was only a hole in the side of the mountain, leading nowhere.

'Oh well, that's just too bad,' sighed George, after she too had searched every inch of the cave. 'We might as well give up!'

The Five came out of the dark cave and back into the sunlight again. It was a hot day, and the sun was beating down on the path outside. Their eyes were dazzled at first, and they bumped into two figures whose outlines they could hardly make out.

'Hallo, what's this?' asked a rough voice. 'Looks like a bunch of kids!'

'What are you lot doing here?' asked another voice, sounding as unfriendly as the first one.

Now that their eyes were used to the daylight again, the Five could make out the figures of two tall youths in rough, untidy clothes. They seemed to be about eighteen or nineteen, and they didn't look nice at all!

Chapter Four

IVOR AND PHIL

'Golly — I wouldn't like to meet *them* on a dark night!' thought Dick to himself, and he was not a timid boy.

George boldly stepped forward to face the two strangers.

'Good afternoon!' she said. Her tone of voice was a real lesson in politeness all by itself! 'What are we doing here? Well, the same as you, I expect, going for a walk!'

There was a nasty glint in the taller youth's eyes.

'Hear what that lad says, Ivor?' he asked his companion. 'Cheeky he is, indeed!'

It wasn't by any means the first time that someone had taken George for a boy, and usually she was rather pleased. This time, however, she hardly noticed. There was something that struck her as vaguely threatening in the attitude of these two strangers. Timmy seemed to feel the same. He was standing beside her. He didn't growl, but the hairs on the back of his neck were bristling.

'I wasn't being cheeky,' said George. 'Just answering your question!'

'Chatty, too!' said the youth addressed as Ivor. 'What do you say we make him sing a bit less, Phil?'

Phil was smiling unpleasantly.

'Let's hear his little friends answer my question first! What are you kids doing here?'

Julian looked him straight in the eye. 'Going for a walk, as my cousin Georgina has already told you,' he said.

'We're climbing Mount Graig!' Anne explained, overcoming her secret terror of these two tall young fellows.

'Oh, so this isn't a boy at all!' said Ivor, looking at George. 'Going for a walk, is it, indeed? We saw you come out of that little cave. Poking and prying!'

'Poking and prying or not, we've got a perfect right to go for a walk!' said Dick, who was getting fed up with all this.

'Let us by!' added George.

'Hey, not so fast, there!' said Phil, stretching out his arm to prevent them going any farther along the path.

But he wasn't reckoning with Timmy! The good dog growled, and he bared his gleaming teeth, rolling the whites of his eyes at Ivor and Phil. He looked as if he'd attack them at any moment.

41

'Take it easy, will you?' said Phil, in alarm.

His friend tugged at his sleeve. 'Come on, let's be off! I don't like the look of that brute!'

'Oh, all right,' said Phil. 'Okay, kids – but mind you don't cross our path again!'

'I don't see why not,' muttered George, patting Timmy while the two disreputable-looking young men walked off towards the village.

'They were pretty unpleasant, weren't they?' said Dick.

'I hope we *don't* meet them again!' cried Anne.

Julian was looking thoughtful. 'They're not tourists,' he said. 'They spoke with a Welsh accent. It looks as if they live near here, so it seems more than likely that we *shall* be seeing more of them if we go on with our explorations in search of the lost valley.'

'Who cares?' said George. '*I'm* not scared of them! They look to me stupid and lazy as well as bad-tempered. If they bother us, good old Timmy here will make mincemeat of them. You'd gobble them right up, wouldn't you, Tim?'

'I should think he'd find them rather tough!' said Julian, smiling.

'And they might give him food poisoning, poor thing!' added Dick.

These little jokes made the children feel better, and they went on climbing the mountain, forgetting all about Phil and Ivor.

They explored really thoroughly all afternoon, but their efforts were not rewarded. They didn't find out anything new, and although they examined the steep and rocky right-hand part of the slope carefully, over quite a large part of its area, there wasn't any oddity about it so far as they could see.

However, searching so closely, they hadn't climbed very far before it was time to go down again.

'This exploration looks like taking us ages,' said Dick. 'I'll probably have a long white beard by the time we get to the top!'

'Yes, and there's another thing,' added his brother. 'Even when we do get to the top, we'll only have been able to examine the part of the mountainside that's fairly close to the path. Supposing the entrance to the valley really does exist, it might be somewhere else – anywhere else, and this is a big mountain!'

'Might as well be searching for a needle in a haystack,' said Dick, gloomily.

'Oh, don't be so depressing!' said George. 'There's no fun in doing anything that comes too easily, is there?'

'No!' said Anne, rather unexpectedly backing her cousin up. 'I'm sure we'll find what we're looking for!'

And the others could tell from her voice that she really *was* sure – she was so fascinated by the legend that she was simply longing to see the truth of it confirmed.

Dick smiled. '*I* think the main thing about our

explorations is to amuse ourselves! If they seem to be more trouble than they're worth, we can always give them up.'

Several times over the next few days, that was what the children felt like doing. They climbed a little higher up the mountain every afternoon, but they hadn't found anything yet, and all of them except George were beginning to get a little tired of the idea. After all, they could be going off to visit the beautiful old castles of Wales instead, or taking bus and coach trips to other interesting places.

What was more, they had bumped into Phil and Ivor again, twice. The two youths were as suspicious and rude as before – and rather threatening too. George and her cousins couldn't really see why they should be so hostile. There didn't seem to be any reason for it.

'Maybe they felt we'd be in their way here on Mount Graig,' said George.

'I can't think why!' said Dick. 'Goodness knows the mountain's big enough for all of us!'

However, it was unpleasant knowing that the two youths resented their explorations. They even seemed to be watching the children from a distance to see what they were up to.

One fine afternoon the Five were starting off on another exploration, not feeling too hopeful by now. Timmy was the only one as full of high spirits as ever. He was gambolling about, sniffing at rabbit-holes, investigating the insects that lived on the mountainside, or rolling on the grass. Suddenly

George saw him get up, sniff the air – and then start off in hot pursuit of a little fieldmouse!

'Stop it, Timmy!' she shouted angrily. 'Leave that poor little mouse alone!'

But just for once Timmy didn't obey his young mistress. He probably imagined he was chasing something fierce and being very brave! Anyway, he went on running straight ahead with his nose to the ground as he chased the mouse. It plunged into a clump of grass and disappeared in a thicket of bushes. Timmy followed, and the bushes closed again after him. There was a rustling of leaves, and then silence.

'Oh no!' said Dick, crossly. 'Now where's Timmy got to?'

George parted the bushes again, calling, 'Tim!, Timmy, old boy!'

Timmy answered her, but with a muffled bark, as if he were a long way off. George plunged through the bushes herself.

'Oh, look!' she exclaimed. 'A cave!'

Sure enough, she had uncovered the entrance to a cave which could not be seen at all from the pathway. It was completely covered by all the green leaves in front of it.

Julian, Dick and Anne were quick to follow their cousin inside.

'Hurray!' cried Dick. 'It's a cave all right – and a bigger one than that disappointing little cave we found the other day. Oh, I bet the way into the lost valley is –'

'I wouldn't bet too much on it!' George told him. 'Look, the grass has been trodden underfoot. You can still see the traces of footprints. Obviously quite a lot of people know about this cave.'

'Oh, look!' cried Anne.

Her eyes had become accustomed to the dim light in the cave, and she was pointing at a collection of objects which were either hanging from rocky outcrops or lying on the floor of the cave. Dick bent down to see what they were.

'Traps – snares – and rabbit-skins being cured! There's a pile of cured skins in that corner, too.'

'It looks as if this is a poacher's hideout,' said Julian.

'Well, that explains everything!' said George, with a certain amount of triumph in her voice. 'I *thought* as much! So that's why Ivor and Phil didn't like having us here! They were afraid we might discover what they were up to, and find their hiding-place for the game they poach!'

'I think you're right,' said Dick. 'Yes – they must be poachers!'

'Well, it could be somebody else,' Julian pointed out. 'We don't have any proof that Ivor and Phil are the ones who've been setting these snares.'

However, proof was what he was just about to get!

There was a rustle of leaves behind the children. Julian turned his head. Anne let out a squeal of terror! Ivor and Phil had just come into the cave.

'I told you those kids were still spying on us!'

46

said Phil. 'Didn't believe me, did you? Well, there's no more doubt about it now!'

Those words certainly gave *him* away. As for the children, *they* were in no more doubt that the two youths were poachers. Ivor stepped forward, looking very threatening.

'You'd better watch out – no going to the police, d'you hear?' he said in a nasty voice. 'Because you'll be sorry if you do give us away!'

George was having difficulty in keeping Timmy under control. She just looked scornful.

'We haven't been spying on you,' she said. 'It's simply not the kind of thing we do!'

'So what are you up to here, eh?' asked Phil.

'We're having a holiday in Wales, that's all,' Dick answered back. 'And we're spending our time going for walks and climbs. What's so odd about that?'

'Pretending not to understand my question, are you, then? I want to know what you're up to *here* – in this cave!'

'My dog was running after a fieldmouse, and we followed him in,' George explained truthfully.

However, Ivor and Phil didn't seem to believe her. Anne thought they were looking very frightening, and she lost her head.

'Honestly, my cousin's telling the truth!' she said. 'We only discovered this cave by chance – and it's not the one we're really looking for at all, it's –'

'Shut up, Anne!' said George furiously.

But too late! The damage was done. Ivor and Phil were looking at the little girl with interest.

'Go on!' Phil told her. 'What *was* the one you were looking for, then?'

George was going to let Timmy spring at the youths, but Ivor saw her just in time, and he brought a sharp knife out of his pocket.

'Set that brute of yours on me and I'll kill him!' he threatened.

George kept perfectly still – and Anne talked. Julian looked resigned, and George and Dick looked very angry indeed, as the poor little girl told the poachers why they were exploring the mountainside. When she had finished her story, Phil burst out laughing.

'You silly bunch of kids! Nobody believes that legend of the Dark Folk any more! Well, you just carry on searching for the lost valley if you like – but I'm warning you again, don't tell a living soul what we're up to. And don't let us find you getting underfoot again! Get out now, will you?'

Fuming, but glad to have got away so lightly, the children left the poachers' hideout and walked away in silence.

Phil and Ivor watched them go. Then they turned to look at each other.

'Hey – suppose that story *was* true?' said Ivor thoughtfully. 'Suppose there really is a golden statue? Those kids seem determined to discover it!'

'Then let them do the work for us, Ivor! And if they happen to come across it, we'll nip in and get it from them. Meanwhile, better keep an eye on them.'

'Yes,' agreed Ivor. 'What a joke if they led us to the treasure!'

Delighted with this idea, the two youths set happily to work to do up a bundle of rabbit-skins!

And over the next few days the Five went on with their patient explorations – never guessing that they were being watched themselves.

Much to their disappointment, they explored all the way to the top of Mount Graig, and still found nothing. That evening Julian suggested giving up the whole project and thinking of something else to do while they were at Magga Glen.

'Let's see how we feel tomorrow,' said George. 'We'll sleep on it before we decide!'

But as luck would have it, nobody was going to sleep on anything much that night!

Chapter Five

ALARMS IN THE NIGHT

What happened in the night was going to make a lot of difference to the Five's Welsh holiday.

Everyone in Magga Glen farmhouse was peacefully asleep when a violent shock awoke them between four and five in the morning. The children were thrown almost to the ends of their beds. Anne woke with a start, and couldn't help crying out in terror, 'George – oh, George, what's going on?'

George was in the next bed. She tried to put a light on, but although Mrs Jones had had electricity installed in the farmhouse since the children's last visit, it wasn't working now. There was another funny sort of shock, and Anne screamed again.

'My word!' said George, rather awed. 'I think it's an earth tremor! Quick, Anne – grab some clothes and let's hurry out into the garden. It's not a good idea to stay indoors.'

Bravely overcoming her terror, Anne did as George said. There was a lot of noise in the farmhouse now. The girls could hear Mrs Jones talking to her son, Morgan, in Welsh, and Morgan was replying in his deep, booming voice. Footsteps came along the corridor, and Aunt Fanny and Uncle Quentin appeared in the doorway of the girls' bedroom. They were carrying torches.

'George – Anne!' cried Aunt Fanny. 'Are you all right? Quick – out into the garden! The boys are there already! Hurry up!'

'Woof!' said Timmy, obediently running to the door.

Outside, the night air was quite warm. There was not a breath of wind. But it seemed as if the earth was shaking slightly underfoot all the time.

'The best place to stand is the middle of the lawn,' said Uncle Quentin. 'We'll be in no danger from falling masonry there!'

'Oh, I hope there *isn't* any falling masonry!' said Aunt Fanny. 'I wouldn't like to think of poor Mrs Jones and Morgan having their house damaged – and all our things are inside it, too!'

George was more interested than alarmed. 'I say, Father – until we were talking to old Branwen the other day, I thought we didn't *have* earthquakes in the British Isles!' she said.

'Well, I'm afraid you were wrong there, George,' Uncle Quentin told her. 'But usually they are so slight that nobody really notices them. However, there is occasionally a tremor or series of

tremors that does damage — and I'm told that's happened several times over the centuries here in Magga Glen. As you may know, the Welsh mountains are composed of volcanic rock from very ancient times. Well, when they formed just here, apparently it was over a fault in the earth's crust, and that is what causes earthquakes — or their little cousins, earth tremors.'

There was a slight rumbling sound which seemed to come from underground, and Uncle Quentin interrupted his explanation to say, 'Lie down, everyone: you'll be safer then!'

The earth certainly *was* shaking under them! The children and Aunt Fanny all did as Uncle Quentin said. The tremor didn't last long, but Timmy wasn't enjoying it at all, and kept growling as if he were telling it to stop!

'Well, well, well!' said Uncle Quentin, getting to his feet as the tremor died away. 'Fascinating! Really fascinating! What remarkable luck that we happened to be in Wales just now — that must have been one of the biggest earth tremors recorded in the British Isles!'

'Luck, did you say?' repeated Aunt Fanny faintly. She didn't share her husband's detached scientific interest!

The occupants of Magga Glen Farm all waited out in the garden for some time longer, but evidently the earth tremors were over. Alarming as they had been, there was no damage to the farmhouse except that a crack in one wall had got rather larger. Morgan examined it and thought it would be quite easy to repair.

Day was beginning to dawn, and Uncle Quentin and Morgan Jones decided to go down to the village and see if anybody there needed help. 'We may be able to be useful,' said Uncle Quentin.

The children insisted on coming too. It wasn't likely they'd get any more sleep if they went back to bed! So they got dressed and set off with Morgan and Uncle Quentin down the road to Magga Glen village. Several of the cottages here *had* suffered a little damage – slates had come off rooftops, and there were cracks in several whitewashed walls. Part of the little church tower had actually fallen down, but luckily nobody was badly hurt. However, there were several scratches and bruises, and the children helped the district nurse give first aid, and joined in the tidying-up. Their friend old Branwen the storyteller had had all her kitchen utensils thrown off their shelves and jumbled about by the earth tremor, and as her poor old hands were so rheumaticky the children cleared everything up for her. Timmy wasn't much real use, but now he had got over his fright at the earth tremor he was very interested in the unusual excitement about the place, and went round poking his nose into everything!

When there was nothing more they could do in the village, Uncle Quentin, Morgan Jones and the Five went back to the farmhouse, where Mrs Jones had a huge and delicious breakfast waiting for them. Aunt Fanny had been helping her to cook lots of bacon and eggs and sausages, and there was a big loaf of crusty bread with butter and home-made strawberry jam, with cool, creamy milk for the children and a pot of really strong tea for the grown-ups.

'This is scrumptious!' said Dick, helping himself to a second plateful of eggs and bacon. 'I think breakfast tastes even *better* after an earth tremor!'

'We can be doing without too many of them, thank you, lad!' said Morgan Jones with a twinkle in his eye.

Somehow the excitement of the earth tremor had taken the children's minds off their exploration of the mountainside. They stayed near Magga Glen Farm all day – they *were* a little tired after being woken up so early, and then working hard helping the villagers to clear up.

Next day, however, everything seemed to be back to normal, and they decided that before giving up Mount Graig for good, they would go back for one last climb. And when they got there, there was a surprise waiting for them!'

They had been climbing for a little while when Timmy, who was bounding on ahead of the children, suddenly stopped dead and began to bark.

'I think he's found something!' said George. She ran on to join the dog, and Julian, Dick and Anne hurried after her.

When they all arrived at the spot, Timmy was

standing perfectly still, sniffing at a deep crack that had appeared right across the path.

'The earth tremor must have made it!' said Anne.

'It's only a superficial fault,' said Dick, bending over the crack. 'No deeper than a ditch, and nothing like as wide. All we have to do is jump across it.'

'Hang on – we're about level with the little cave we discovered when we began exploring, aren't we?' said Julian. 'I'm sure I recognise this place!'

'Yes, we are,' agreed George. 'Oh, look – the cave itself has gone! Along with the bracken that was hiding it!' And she pointed to a jumble of fallen rocks that stood where the entrance to the little cave had once been. 'So the earth tremor shook the mountainside too!' she observed. Her eyes were shining. 'Let's go and take a look!'

'Take a look at what?' asked Julian.

'At whatever's beyond those rocks! You never know your luck!'

It wasn't at all difficult for the children to move a few of the rocks aside – and they could see that something had happened to the little cave beyond them, making it bigger.

'But we'd better not go in,' said the cautious Julian. 'Suppose the whole roof of the cave fell in? It could be dangerous.'

'Anyway, we've already explored this cave,' said Dick, rather bored.

However, George already *had* disappeared into

the cave – and a moment later her cousins heard her shouting triumphantly. In spite of Julian's warnings, all the others ran in after her, Julian himself included. They found her standing at the back of the cave looking at a large crack in the rocky wall. She was shining her torch on to it.

'See that?' she asked. 'The earth tremor made an opening here – and I can feel air coming through it from behind! This could be the way into the secret valley!'

A moment later a strange little procession was making its way through the new opening in the wall at the back of the cave. It was led by George, lighting up the way for the others. She was the only one who had thought of putting a torch in her pocket when they set off – and unfortunately the battery was beginning to run rather low.

The opening itself stretched a long way up-wards, but was only just wide enough for the children to squeeze through – luckily none of them was at all fat! Even Dick stayed as thin as a rake in spite of his huge appetite. At first the Five had to pick their way through bits of fallen rock, but after they had gone a few yards the going was easier.

'It looks as if this tunnel's always been here,' said Dick. 'Only its entrance was blocked up! It seems to go right into the heart of the mountain.'

'We've got to be careful,' Julian told the others. 'We have no idea where it leads – and we don't know exactly what the earth tremor has done. We might step down into a hole any moment, or set off a fall of rocks to land on our heads!'

'I suppose you're right,' George admitted. 'But we may be on the point of finding the way into the lost valley – and discovering the secrets of the Dark Folk!'

And she walked determinedly on. She put great faith in Timmy's instinct for danger – she was sure he'd warn them of any risks that lay ahead. Dick was as adventurous as his cousin, and followed her very willingly. Julian was worried when he realised that the light of their only torch was getting very faint, but he knew they must all keep together. Anne kept close to him. She didn't like this at all – she was afraid of spraining an ankle falling over one of the rocks that were scattered about the floor of the tunnel.

Then, all of a sudden, George's torch went right out.

'Oh no!' groaned four disappointed voices in the dark.

Chapter Six

ADVENTURES UNDERGROUND

'Told you so!' said Julian, which was very annoying for the others.

'Bother!' said George, shaking her torch. It came on again, but the light was very feeble. 'I suppose we'll have to turn back! This wretched torch has just enough power left in the battery to show us the way.'

In fact the torch gave hardly any light, and the young explorers hurried along the underground passage as fast as they could, so as to get out into the cave before the battery went completely dead on them. They just made it, and emerged into the light of day again.

'Phew!' said Dick, heaving a deep sigh of relief.

'We'd better come back here with new batteries,' said Julian. 'We could have been running a lot of danger in there without proper light to see by!'

George was looking thoughtfully at the mouth of

the cave. Timmy was imitating her. He looked very funny with his head on one side, just like his little mistress!

'Listen, we can't leave the place looking like this!' said George abruptly. 'Suppose somebody else came along and found the tunnel, they might get to the lost valley ahead of us! We ought to camouflage the mouth of this cave – pile up rocks in front of it.'

'You're right,' Julian agreed. 'It won't take us long if we all lend a hand.'

Sure enough, the work was soon done – and as it turned out, just in time! For the children had only just finished when they heard footsteps coming along the path.

Ivor and Phil appeared round the corner. They had probably been up to the cave which they used as a hideout for their poaching equipment.

'Hallo – our nosey little friends!' said Phil. 'Well, still going for walks with clever ideas in your heads?'

'Not too frightened the other night, were you?' asked Ivor mockingly. 'That tremor gave Magga Glen a shaking, didn't it, now?'

The children said nothing. They couldn't stand these unpleasant, dishonest youths, and they weren't going to rise to the bait of their teasing!

However, Phil had a naturally quarrelsome nature, and their silence made him crosser than ever. He frowned. 'Lost your tongues? Can't you answer a civil question, then?'

'We might if it *was* a civil one!' said George, shortly. 'We haven't told the police about you, if that's what you're wondering! But we don't much want to talk to you, so you just go your way and let us go ours!'

George had many good qualities, such as honesty, courage and generosity – but no one could have said that tact was among them! Her answer really annoyed Phil. He went red in the face with anger, clenched his fists, and snarled, 'I've a good mind to give you a hiding, boy!'

'She's a girl, not a boy, remember?' said his friend Ivor, laughing. 'Wouldn't hit a girl, would you, Phil? Ha, ha, ha!'

George felt her own temper wearing thin. She was about to answer back sharply when Julian prudently intervened.

'Let's not argue,' he said, raising one hand in an appeasing gesture.

But unfortunately, that hand was all dirty from the earth that had been sticking to the rocks he and the others had moved, and Phil noticed it at once.

'Hey, look at that!' he said, forgetting about George. 'Why, anyone'd say you kids had been moving rocks about! You've *all* got dirty hands, haven't you, now? Well, well! Maybe you discovered something new? And if you did, well, we'd really like to know about it, yes indeed!'

George trembled: she felt sure the two poachers would like to get their hands on the golden statue, supposing it really existed, and Phil was already looking hopefully at Anne. He knew she was the weakest of the Five – hadn't she already given them some very useful information? Poor little Anne was so frightened she looked as if she would faint on the spot with fear!

The blood rose to George's head. 'That's quite enough of that!' she said. 'You just leave us alone, or you'll be sorry – go on, Timmy, get them!'

This time Ivor and Phil did not have knives in their hands, and they were taken by surprise. They suddenly found themselves being attacked by a furious whirlwind! Once George had given him the word, Timmy went for them, racing round and round them so fast that all Ivor and Phil could see of him was his shining teeth, his bloodshot eyes, his wide-open jaws and the bristling hairs on his back. Timmy bit one of them in the calf, had a nip at the other's ankle, snapped at a sleeve here and a pair of trousers there – he seemed to be in several places all at once.

It was too much for the young poachers! They ran off as fast as they could go. It was not a very glorious retreat – and Timmy helped them on their way by chasing after them, barking triumphantly. George was laughing so much she could hardly get enough breath back to call him off.

'Here, Tim – heel! Good dog! Well done, old chap!'

She found a sugar lump in her pocket as a reward for him. Her cousins all hugged the good dog. But Julian was still rather worried: this was a real declaration of war between the Five and the poachers! Who knew what they might do now?

Next day the Five set off back to the cave, armed with brand-new batteries in their torches. Julian, who always thought of everything, brought a stick of chalk and a ball of string along too.

'The underground passage may fork somewhere or other,' he explained. 'If it does, we won't want to run the risk of getting lost. We can make marks on the rocks with the chalk to help us find our way back.'

'What's the string for?' asked Anne

'Well, that's in case things get even more complicated. If we tie the end of the string to a piece of rock and unwind the ball as we go along, then we simply can't get lost! Remember the story of Theseus and the Minotaur? It's an even better safety measure than the chalk marks.'

'Why?' asked Anne again.

'Because you need light to see chalk marks – and you can do without any if you're using the string.'

'But we've got our torches!' the little girl objected.

'They might go out.'

'We've put in new batteries. They should last several hours!'

'All the same, torches can break if you drop them.'

'We'd all four of us have to be *very* clumsy at one and the same time!' Dick told his brother, laughing. 'Come off it, Ju – or should I say Theseus?

You're going a bit too far!'

'Precautions are always a good thing,' Julian insisted, 'and the more of them the better!'

'In fact, you're the sort who always wears belt *and* braces!' said Dick, and this time even Julian had to laugh.

As they chatted, the Five had reached the place where they had had to turn back the day before. But now they could go on, thanks to the bright light from their torches. They made quite fast progress along the underground tunnel. Its floor was fairly smooth and level.

George was leading the way, and as she was really quite a sensible girl at heart, she was being as careful as even Julian could have wished. Her heart was beating fast. They might come upon something exciting any moment now!

Suddenly the tunnel ahead of her grew wider.

'Look – another cave!' she cried.

Julian, Dick, Anne and Timmy came hurrying up. They found themselves in a large natural cave, which must have been dug into the rock by currents of water in ancient, primaeval times.

'Gosh – look at this!' said Dick, shining his torch on the cave wall closest to him. 'There are pictures here!'

George looked at them in amazement. 'My word, yes – cave paintings!'

The pictures showed men armed with primitive weapons hunting game – birds and animals.

'Huntsmen!' said Anne. 'Huntsmen with their

dogs!'

'And they have dark faces,' Dick pointed out delightedly.

'Golly – could these be the Dark Folk themselves?' Julian wondered. For once he seemed quite shaken. 'I say – this may be a really important discovery!'

'It's marvellous!' cried George. '*Now* do you think we're on a wild goose chase, Ju, looking for the lost valley?'

'Hang on,' said Julian. 'These cave paintings may be nothing to do with the Dark Folk – they could be from a different period. Uncle Quentin would know, I expect.'

'Well, anyway, they prove that people *did* use this cave, and the tunnel leading to it,' said George.

'Let's explore the cave,' Anne suggested.

They found a great many more cave paintings. It was all most exciting! And they made another discovery, too – two more underground passages came out in the cave, one to their right, quite close to the passage along which they had come, and another to their left, at the far side of the cave.

The children looked at each other, baffled.

'Well, all roads may lead to Rome, but I don't suppose all underground tunnels lead to the lost valley,' said George. 'So which shall we try?'

'First one and then the other,' said Anne, sensibly enough.

But George and Dick were in a great hurry now. 'Let's divide up into two teams,' said George.

'That doubles our chances of success!'

Julian was not so sure about this, but at last he agreed. He and Anne made up one team, and Dick, George and Timmy were the other.

'We'd better fix a definite time,' said Julian. 'Let's say we go on walking for half an hour, and then retrace our steps and come back here.'

Once they had all agreed to this, the two teams set off in different directions. Julian and Anne went down the passage on the right, and George, Dick and Timmy set off along the tunnel at the other side of the cave with the pictures on its walls.

Timmy was leading the second party, running happily ahead of the two cousins and wagging his tail. 'That's a good sign!' George decided. 'I'm sure he's got wind of something!'

Dick was not quite so certain, but still, it seemed hopeful.

And it *was* Timmy who was first to their next big find. Several paces ahead of George, tail wagging quite frantically now, he came out into a large room-like cave. This one had evidently been hewn out of the rock by the hand of man. The two children shouted for joy at the sight before them.

'It's amazing!' cried Dick. 'George, this looks like a sort of – a sort of a crypt or something, don't you think? Look, there's a stone altar, and stone benches –'

'And some old, old dishes that look like primitive oil lamps!' said George, running to examine the little lamps standing on ledges at different points of the room.

She and Dick both explored the place, shining their torches on the walls, and uttering exclamations of surprise and delight whenever they found some new, fascinating discovery.

'Well, that *proves* it!' said George at last, triumphantly. 'Whether it was the Dark Folk or not, people did live in these underground caves. They worshipped some kind of god or gods here, and they left pictures of their daily lives on the walls.'

'Woof!' commented Timmy. He had disappeared behind the stone altar.

Dick and George went to look for him – and found themselves facing the entrance of another cave, directly behind the altar, which had been hiding it.

Dick looked at his watch. 'We haven't got time to look at it now!' he told his cousin. 'The half-hour's nearly up – we'd better go back to Julian and Anne.'

Julian and Anne were waiting in the cave with the paintings, looking rather impatient.

'Nothing to report!' Julian told the others at once. 'We've been back here for some time.'

'Yes,' sighed Anne. 'We were getting quite tired of waiting for you!'

Julian finished the story of what he and Anne had found – it was quite a short one, because they hadn't found much! 'First we went up quite a steep slope, then the passage turned a corner, and our way was barred almost at once by a wall of rock. There wasn't a hope of getting past it or round it, so we had to retrace our steps.'

'Well, we had better luck!' said George, and she told the others what she and Dick had found.

'That's terrific!' said Julian. 'Show us!'

He and Anne followed George and Dick, who were delighted to show off 'their' crypt. This time even Julian was convinced that a group or tribe of people who had long since vanished from the face of the earth must have lived in these dark caverns, many centuries ago.

Next day the children armed themselves with more new torch batteries from one of the village shops in Magga Glen – they were spending a fortune on batteries, but it was worth it! They had decided to explore even farther. Where did the opening behind the stone altar lead?

They set off with great enthusiasm. But things didn't go quite so easily that day.

Chapter Seven

SOME PROBLEMS

For a start, the Five met the two young poachers right at the foot of Mount Graig. They looked as if they were waiting about on purpose to see the children. Ivor was cleaning his nails with the point of his knife – they *needed* cleaning, but George and her cousins didn't like the look of that knife! Phil had a riding whip in his hand. George realised that they were well armed against Timmy – if he attacked them again, he'd probably come off worst this time.

'Here, Timmy!' she said quietly to her dog. 'Heel! Stay with me – good dog!'

Anne looked at the two unpleasant fellows, feeling very worried. She might have a timid nature, but she was able to overcome her fear and even be quite brave at times – just now, however, she couldn't think *what* the four of them and Timmy could do, and she looked like a frightened little animal that had been hunted down.

However, it seemed that the young poachers were not going to try to stop the exploration party! All they did was to follow the Five, at a distance – although they obviously didn't intend to lose sight of them. In the circumstances, thought George, they couldn't possibly go back to the cave.

Anne was the first to break the glum silence that had fallen. She had a clever idea, too! 'Exactly where do those wild flowers grow, George?' she asked her cousin. 'The ones Aunt Fanny asked us to pick her, I mean! I can't see many here.'

George immediately realised what a fine way Anne was suggesting of leading the enemy off the scent – and *with* scent, too: the scent of flowers!

'Oh, higher up!' she said. '*Much* higher up – that's where the best flowers grow! We'll have to climb quite a way yet.'

So up they climbed – and they spent several hours picking flowers, lying about on the short-cropped grass in the sun, and running races with Timmy. Ivor and Phil looked more and more bored and annoyed as they hung about where they could watch the children.

As they cycled home again that evening, George said, 'Well, we played a good trick on those two louts! But it doesn't get us much farther. If they're going to watch us the whole time, we'll never manage to do any more exploration. How infuriating!'

And her annoyance increased the next day, and the day after that. Because sure enough, the two poachers *were* determined to follow the Five, even if they weren't quite so obvious about it as they had been on the first day. Their clumsy efforts at shadowing the children soon had everyone's nerves on edge.

'We'll have to give it up for the time being!' said Julian in disgust.

'Oh no!' protested George. 'We'd be losing so much time – after all, we're not going to spend the *whole* holidays in Wales!' She sounded so doleful that her cousins couldn't help smiling, remembering how she hadn't wanted to come in the first place! 'Why don't we go to the caves by night?'

'Oh, my goodness – Aunt Fanny and Uncle Quentin would *never* let us do that!' gasped Anne.

'Well, we don't have to tell them, do we?' laughed Dick. He thought his cousin's idea was an excellent one.

'I didn't actually mean at night so much as in the evening,' George explained. 'And we wouldn't go every evening, of course. I say, Ju, you could take your camera and flashlight and photograph those wonderful cave paintings!'

That was clever of George – she knew it was a temptation Julian couldn't resist! He had a fine new camera, and he had already mentioned the possibility of taking it into the caves with them. The thought of taking photographs soon got him to agree to his cousin's plan.

The children were a little uneasy when they set off on their first evening expedition. They didn't like the idea of deceiving Aunt Fanny and Uncle Quentin by going off in secret – and Timmy seemed to be infected by their mood, and was rather uneasy himself.

Once they were on the path leading up to the cave the Five kept very much on the alert. Ivor and Phil probably went poaching after dark! So there was the chance of running into them at any moment.

However, they reached the cave with the paintings easily enough, and Julian took lots of photos of the hunters, and of another fresco showing musicians and dancers in flowing robes.

'Now let's go on exploring!' said George.

The Five lost no time in hurrying along the passage leading to the crypt-like cave and starting down the tunnel that began behind the altar there. Julian had brought the torches with their new batteries, but he still insisted on unwinding his ball of string behind them. He felt rather uncomfortable, although he was not sure why – perhaps it was because they had come out here after dark, without permission from Aunt Fanny and Uncle Quentin.

The children went about twenty metres down the new tunnel, and then suddenly found themselves facing a place where it forked in two, making a Y shape with the part along which they had just come.

'Let's divide up, the way we did before,' suggested Dick.

'No,' said Julian. 'I think we'd better stick together this time.'

George didn't object, and they all set off along the right-hand tunnel. Unfortunately it came to a dead end after only a few more metres, so they turned round and retraced their footsteps. Then they tried the left-hand tunnel. They went along it in silence. Julian's feeling of uneasiness was increasing all the time.

'If Uncle Quentin notices we're not in our bedrooms – ' he began, but an exclamation from George cut him short.

'Oh no!' cried George, in dismay. '*Another* dead end!'

She was leading the little procession, and she had suddenly come up against another blank wall. She and her cousins stared at the rock face before them. It was very disappointing.

'So that's it!' sighed Dick. 'We *can't* get any farther. This is the end of our adventure.'

'Let's go home to bed,' said Anne.

'Go home?' protested George. 'Not yet! I don't believe the trail can really end here! We have proof that there *were* people living in these caves in the mountain, but we can only have found some of their tunnels and caverns so far. There must be more! We haven't found the lost valley itself yet – the place where the Dark Folk were supposed to have built their settlement!'

She suddenly stopped talking. Her cousin Anne was behaving rather oddly! She looked as if she were attending to something else – and Timmy, who was standing beside the little girl, seemed to be listening hard too.

'What's up, Anne?' asked Dick.

'Ssh!' whispered Anne. 'Come here and put your ears to this rock wall. Can you hear anything?'

'Why, yes!' cried Julian. 'A sort of dull, roaring sound.'

'Like rushing water!' added George.

'That must be it!' said Dick. 'The roaring water! Don't you remember – the valley and the settlement in it were both called "Temulka" – a name meaning "roaring water"!'

'Then the lost valley is behind this wall!' said George calmly, feeling very confident now.

Julian himself was half convinced. But the wall of rock was still in their way, and they had no means of getting past it! It was a really massive slab of stone, and there was no chance at all that four children and a dog could push it over.

There was nothing they could do but go back to Magga Glen farmhouse.

They woke up rather later than usual next day. They were feeling just a little ashamed of going out without permission last night – and they were a bit tired too. The children decided not to repeat the expedition that evening.

It was a rather rainy day, and mist swirled about the hills and the mountain peaks. Luckily the children had brought plenty of games and books with them. They spent the day quietly indoors, and tried to decide what to do next about their explorations. Was it time to tell the grown-ups what they'd already found? A team of workmen could probably get through that wall of rock! And then they would have no more to fear from Ivor and Phil.

Julian and Anne thought that was the best solution. Dick hadn't made his mind up – and George was against it!

'We ought to make one *last* try ourselves,' she said. 'Let's have another look at that slab of rock. It seemed to be perfectly smooth and bare, didn't it? And it's blocking the way into the valley. What I wonder is, could it possibly be a kind of swinging or pivoting door? One we could open if we could only find the right place to press?'

After a good deal of discussion, she persuaded her cousins to risk a final effort next day. They'd see if they couldn't get past that slab of rock somehow!

'We can go there in daylight,' George decided. 'I don't think Ivor and Phil will be following us any more – if they *have* been following us every day recently they must be jolly well fed up by now! I'm sure they think we've given up.'

So next day the Five set off quite early, taking a picnic with them. The weather had cleared, and it was a lovely day. The sun shone brightly down as the children approached Mount Graig. They didn't go through the village itself, just in case they happened to meet the two poachers, but went the longer way round it and then joined the path leading up the mountainside again. They climbed on in silence until they reached the little cave.

Julian, Dick and George hurried through the vegetation hiding the mouth of the cave, while Anne took a last look behind her. The little girl wasn't terribly happy – she felt as if invisible eyes were watching every move they made! But Timmy seemed to be quite at ease, and that was reassuring.

Once the Five were inside the little cave they piled up stones in the entrance to the tunnel behind them – they knew they mustn't take risks. Then they hurried along the tunnel itself, and went through the cave with the paintings and the crypt-like cavern. Finally, they went down the tunnel that came to a dead end in the wall of rock.

'Now what?' said Dick, looking at the great slab gloomily. 'I suppose we could always say "Open Sesame!" to it, like Ali Baba! Got anything better to suggest, George?'

'Yes – I suggest you shut up and help me take a good look at it!' said his cousin.

The tunnel had widened as it approached the slab of rock, so there was room for all the children to have a go at it. George and her cousins felt sure it *was* some kind of secret door, and they pushed it and pressed it in all sorts of different places. But it was no good! Whether they pushed it on the right or the left, or even in the middle, not that that seemed a very hopeful idea, nothing happened at all. The slab of rock didn't budge by so much as the

fraction of an inch!

The children were perspiring and feeling discouraged, and they were just going to give up when Timmy, who was snuffling about after some little animal as usual, suddenly happened to bump his nose into the rock down at ground level.

All at once there was a sort of little click, and the huge slab of rock rose in the air, swinging upwards just like a garage door.

Chapter Eight

THE ROARING WATER

The children let out exclamations of amazement! They were facing a huge opening, and they only had to step forward to find themselves on the other side of the rock wall. George and Dick were already on the move!

'Wait!' said Julian firmly. 'Suppose the rock closes behind us again? We'd be caught like rats in a trap. We must have a good look at the way it opens and shuts before we venture any farther in!'

He was quite right, of course, and George felt a little ashamed of herself for not thinking of that first. She could see it was a wise precaution.

It turned out to be perfectly simple to open and close the door. If Julian, who was the tallest of the children, stood on tiptoe, all he had to do was push the front of the stone slab and it swung back down again. It was shaped like a huge rectangle and fitted the end of the tunnel perfectly. They could open it again just by pushing it quite gently close to the ground. And the system worked in exactly the same way on the other side. The children made sure of that before they *all* went through the opening, and carefully closed the 'door' behind them.

Then they set off again, eager to see what lay ahead. The roaring of the water grew louder and louder as they went along. Soon the tunnel went round a corner – and the explorers came out into the lost valley they had been trying so hard to find! They had done it at last!

It had been worth it, too! They felt their efforts were really rewarded. The Five stood there spell-bound, staring at the sight before their eyes.

It really was a kind of valley – a rather narrow, deep one. The children switched off their torches. They didn't need them now, because the strange valley was bathed in a dim green light filtering down through its 'roof' – there was a large crack up above which let in the light of day.

At the moment, the Five were standing on a little rocky rise. They had a good view of the valley around them.

A great waterfall cascaded down into the valley from a natural rock wall on their left. As it reached the ground it became a rushing river. The roaring noise the children had heard was the sound of the waterfall combined with the noise of the torrential river water. Their ears gradually got used to the din. But they all had to shout to make themselves

heard when at last they had recovered from their amazement enough to exchange their first impressions of the place!

'I *say*!' exclaimed Julian. 'See that waterfall!'

'And the river,' said Anne. 'Oh, doesn't it flow fast?'

'So this is the fabulous valley of Temulka!' George marvelled.

'Hurray!' shouted Dick. 'We've found the lost valley!'

'Woof!' agreed Timmy.

At last George tore her eyes away from the foaming waters and looked beyond them.

'My word!' she said. 'I do believe those are houses!'

The underground river was running from left to right, seen from where the Five were standing, and it cut the valley in half. There was nothing but bare rock on the side where the children stood. But there were some very strange buildings on the *other* side of the river! You could tell they had been used as houses, from the number of them and the way they were grouped together. They all had primitive door and window openings, but the most surprising thing about them was their shape. They were built like round towers!

'Gosh! That must be the Dark Folk's settlement!' said Dick, much impressed.

'Come on!' cried George. 'Let's go and take a closer look!'

Led by Timmy, the Five ran down from the little

slope on which they were standing, where the tunnel had come out. It didn't take them long to cross the ground between themselves and the river. But once they reached its bank, there was another question they had to face!

How were they going to get over?

The waterfall and the wall of rock barred their way to the left – and far away on the right, the torrent of water fell through a great crevice in the ground with a roar like thunder, right up against another rock wall. There was no possible chance of getting across the river there – it was far too wide, and the water boiled furiously as it fell.

'Oh, bother!' said Dick. 'How *maddening*! It's a really big river – I say, do you think it's another branch of the underground river we discovered when we were at Magga Glen before, and we rescued old Mrs Thomas from those men at Old Towers?'

'Very likely,' said Julian, rather absent-mindedly.

'Anyway, we daren't try swimming across – the current's far too wild and fast,' said George. Even she had to admit it would be dangerous.

'Yes – we'd be swept away like bits of straw,' Dick agreed.

'You're right,' said Julian. He seemed thoughtful. 'What I'm wondering is, how did the Dark Folk manage to get across to the other bank? I suppose there must once have been a bridge.'

The Five stood on the bank, watching the

rushing water flow past and wishing they could get to the houses on the other side. George was furious. She thought of all the wonderful things they might find in those houses. They weren't so very far away – and yet the children could no more get to them than if they had been on another planet!

Then, suddenly, George clapped her hand to her forehead.

'I've got an idea!' she cried.

'Never!' said Dick. 'George, you astonish me!' But there was admiration in his sarcasm too! He knew that his cousin really did get bright ideas.

'Well, what is it?' asked Julian, in a matter-of-fact voice.

'Wait a moment. I haven't worked it all out yet. And I'm not quite sure if we could do it – come on, everyone! Follow me!'

With these words, she set off at a run towards the waterfall. Julian, Dick and Anne hurried after her, and Timmy was bounding along at her side.

George didn't stop until she was right at the foot of the enormous cascade of water. Then she turned and put her hands round her mouth like a speaking trumpet, so that the others could hear her.

When she explained her idea, it sounded rather a wild one! She told her cousins that she'd read a travel book which said you could sometimes walk *between* a cliff face and the water falling over it, and come to no more harm than getting a bit damp from the spray!

'So let's see if *we* can do it!' she finished. She

marched resolutely right up to the waterfall. Anne felt terrified! The noise was deafening now – but when Dick followed his cousin and looked closely at the rock wall, he let out a shout of triumph. There *was* a way the Five could go, along a little ledge on the rock behind the falling water. George and Timmy were the first to venture over, followed by Dick, and then Julian. Anne came last, holding tight to Julian's hand.

The rock was wet, and rather slippery, so they had to be careful where they put their feet, but it wasn't really so very far to go. Once they reached the other side Timmy happily shook himself – and though the children were wet with the spray of the waterfall, they felt happy and triumphant too. They were over the river at last!

Sensible as ever, Julian suggested a rest and something to eat before they went on. Suddenly the others realised they really *were* hungry, what with all the exercise and the excitement they'd had. They had brought their picnic with them. Mrs Jones's special mutton pasties tasted extra good eaten in the strange surroundings of the lost valley, and they caught water from the waterfall to mix their orange squash.

'If you drink it fast enough, it's still almost fizzy!' said Anne. 'Fizzy orange!'

Julian drank some plain water. 'I think it's best on its own,' he said. 'It tastes of all the mountain streams that must join to fall into this underground river.'

The rest did them good, and they were all ready to go on when George said, 'Now let's explore those houses!'

She really thought this was one of the most thrilling adventures they had ever had!

The valley floor turned out to be larger than you might have thought at first sight. It took the Five a good quarter of an hour to reach the first of the round towers. It was made of blocks of stone cleverly fitted together without any mortar. Old as it obviously was, it didn't seem to be in any danger of falling down.

The explorers' hearts were thumping as they went into this strange house. There was nothing in the way of furniture inside – no remains of chairs or tables or beds. But there was a kind of primitive fireplace with a raised hearth.

'People certainly *did* live here once,' murmured Anne. It was an exciting moment.

'I wonder if they managed to grow anything in this underground valley?' said Dick. 'Fruit and vegetables and so on? It doesn't look as if they got much sunlight.'

'I should think it's more likely they went out through their secret tunnels to hunt and gather food in the mountains,' said Julian.

'Well, now we know one thing,' said George. 'The legend's true! The Dark Folk *were* swept away by a disaster!'

'Swept away by a disaster?' said Dick. 'How can you tell?'

George pointed to the ground. 'Look at that, Dick! There are signs of it here – see that sort of crust of dried mud covering the ground? Did you notice that we've been walking over a crust of earth like this ever since we came down from the higher, rocky part of the valley? Well, it must be covering everything up – and that'll be because the river once overflowed its banks. It must have risen very fast indeed, drowning the poor people who lived in the valley and carrying their bodies away to fall down through the huge crevice at the other end, into a ravine below.'

'I think you're probably right,' said Julian slowly. He bent to look at the ground. 'Yes – we're walking over alluvial silt! That means mud left behind, perhaps long ago, by river water,' he told Anne, seeing his little sister open her mouth to ask a question. 'It tells us the story of the Dark Folk as clearly as any written history book could do!'

Anne looked round her with a shudder. 'Oh, that's horrible! All those people drowned and carried away by the river, falling down and down into its depths! A whole settlement of houses swallowed up!'

'It's possible a few people may have had time to escape,' Julian said kindly. He could tell that his sensitive sister was really upset. 'And I expect they went to live with people living in the mountains outside the valley. Why, some of their descendants may be living in Graig and Magga Glen to this day!'

This idea comforted Anne a bit, but Julian, Dick and George felt quite mournful too as they thought of the disaster that had devastated the valley so many hundreds of years ago. Even Timmy let his ears droop and put his tail between his legs, as if he knew what they were thinking. And it *was* a sad thought.

The children went on, in silence, to have a quick look inside some of the other tower-like buildings. Wherever they went, they found something, however slight, to show that human beings really had lived there before the river rose and drowned them.

'I think we've seen enough for one day,' said George, after a while. 'It must be time to go home!'

Her cousins and Timmy followed her out of the valley and back through the caves and underground tunnels – perhaps it was just that they were tired, but they felt quite relieved to be out in the open on the mountainside again! The discovery they had made was sad as well as exciting. But their spirits rose as they cycled home in the late afternoon sunlight.

'We'll do some more exploring tomorrow!' said George.

'Yes, let's!' agreed Julian. 'And I think we ought to take spades and pickaxes with us. I'm sure Morgan would lend us some tools. With luck we might be able to dig up a few things from the dried mud.'

'It's not just dried, it's had centuries to harden it!' Dick pointed out. 'Excavating it won't be easy.'

'Well, we can always try,' said George.

'And if it's *too* hard we could always moisten it with water from the river,' Anne suggested.

'Good idea!' cried George. 'Yes – let's take that folding canvas bucket we use when we go camping. Well done, Anne – that's really good thinking!'

Anne blushed with pleasure. It wasn't so very often she earned praise from her cousin George! By the time they got back to Magga Glen, she was feeling much happier.

And next day the Five set off for the lost valley again, taking tools borrowed from Morgan Jones with them.

Chapter Nine

GOLD!

They took the same precautions as before, but once they were inside the first cave they made good progress. They knew their way quite well by now, so it didn't take them long to camouflage the way into the first cave, go along the tunnels until they reached the swinging door, close the slab behind them, and come out in the hidden valley again.

Timmy seemed to be very cheerful today. He insisted on going ahead of the children, head held high, like a conquering hero! Anne had suggested taking lightweight plastic raincoats so that they wouldn't get too wet crossing the river behind the waterfall, and the children all put them on just before they made their way across. George even tied a piece of plastic on Timmy's back.

'There!' she said. 'That'll keep your coat nice and dry, old boy!'

When the Five reached the far bank of the

underground river they made for the house that was farthest away. George thought they had the best chance of finding something there – it was only logical to suppose that the deposits of mud would have been slighter the farther they were from the river.

'Take it very gently,' Julian advised them, scraping away at the ground with his pickaxe. He knew that you could damage archaeological finds if you were too rough and energetic. 'Just try light little taps!'

Anne went to fetch some water, and poured it on the dry ground that was the floor of the house. Gradually the crust of mud softened a little, and the children scraped it away with their spades. Dick made the first find! All of a sudden he saw a gleam of gold against the dull metal of his spade.

'Oh, look!' he cried, bending to pick the object up. 'It's a bracelet!'

'It looks like gold,' said George, bending over the large ring her cousin was holding.

'It *is* gold!' said Julian, weighing it in his hand. 'Solid gold, too! My word – a gold bracelet! There's no mistaking it – copper wouldn't be shining like that, not after all this time!'

Feeling encouraged and very excited, the Five went on digging with enthusiasm. Even Timmy seemed to get the idea – he was scratching away at the ground with his claws, concentrating on the job in a very comical way! And in fact he was the second member of the excavating party to dig something up.

'Woof! Woof!' he told the children.

'George, Timmy's found something!' said Anne.

'Here, Timmy – let's see it!' George said. 'Good dog!'

Timmy turned his big, shining eyes on his little mistress and began happily wagging his tail.

Right in front of the dog, still half-buried in the mud, lay a strange and very beautiful gold necklace, with little golden discs dangling from it. George picked it up.

'Golly – this must be worth a small fortune!' she said in awe. She washed it carefully in the canvas bucket of water. 'Look how finely worked it is,' she said. 'It's heavy, too!'

'The Dark Folk certainly used gold pretty lavishly!' remarked Julian. 'They don't seem to have needed to economise!'

'It's the legend again!' said Dick enthusiastically. 'Don't you remember? They were said to be able to make gold!'

'Hm – I don't know about *making* gold,' said Julian, 'but they certainly *worked* it. They were very fine goldsmiths. And they obviously had plenty! Of course, there *is* gold in the hills and mountains of Wales.'

'Yes!' said Anne. 'Isn't the Queen's wedding ring made of Welsh gold?'

'That's right,' her big brother told her. 'Well – perhaps the Dark Folk struck a particularly rich vein of gold here in *this* mountain! That would have given them a very good reason for settling in the secret valley.'

The children went on digging, and found several more things in the same house. There were bits of broken pottery, and household utensils made of carved horn or polished stone. Most of these were still intact.

'This is a wonderful hoard we've found!' said Dick, looking at their collection of finds. 'But I should think we've exhausted this house – let's go on to the next one.'

The Five were so excited by their archaeological work that they hardly stopped to eat their picnic lunch. They found more and more things as they dug on through the afternoon. Julian found a collection of gold amulets hanging from a gold chain, and Anne found a golden earring.

'What are we going to do with all our finds?' Dick wondered. It was nearly time to go home.

'We'd better take the things made of gold with us, and keep them safe until we've found out all we can about the Dark Folk,' George said. 'And we can leave the bits of pottery and the utensils made of horn and bone in one of the towers. But I don't want to let anyone know about our discoveries until we've found out as much as we can! Why – we might even find the golden statue of Zulma. Wouldn't that be marvellous? And then we could reveal the whole story!'

George's eyes were shining at the thought of it. And with or without a golden statue, the Five had done very well already!

They set off for the valley once again the next day, and this time George herself made a very important discovery. She found a bow for a musical instrument, made of solid gold. Of course the gut or horsehair that had been used for the strings of the bow had rotted long ago, but you could easily see what the object was. All the children uttered exclamations of amazement at the sight.

'Gosh – a solid gold bow! That *is* unusual!' said Dick.

'And it certainly goes to show the Dark Folk had plenty of gold,' added Julian.

'They must have been musical too,' said Anne.

'I tell you what,' said George, 'I've been thinking, and I believe these Dark Folk probably were a kind of gypsy tribe, or people related to the gypsies. As Julian said, gypsies originally came from the East. The legend says the Dark Folk had brown skins, and one of the frescoes in the cave with the painted walls shows women dancing in long robes, and musicians with rings in their ears, and gypsies *are* very musical – yes, it all adds up!'

George sat down on the ground to go on with what she was saying, and the others listened with interest, even Timmy!

'Gypsies have always been more or less regarded with suspicion, haven't they, Julian?' she asked.

'Unfortunately yes,' said Julian. 'All through the centuries!'

'Well, suppose this tribe of "Dark Folk" was travelling around – rather earlier, perhaps, than most of the ancestors of today's gypsies. And they had to run away from enemies who were determined to wipe them out, and got all the way to the Welsh mountains! They might easily have thought the secret valley would be a very good hiding place, and so they settled here.'

'It's not a bad idea,' agreed Julian.

'Yes – I'm sure George is right,' said Dick.

They went on digging, and when they looked at their watches and saw it was time to go back to Magga Glen they were feeling very pleased with their day's work. They had dug up so much 'treasure' they they felt sure they would find the golden statue too, sooner or later. By now, anyway, they were convinced that it really did exist.

But they were about to make another find – and this time one that would spoil their pleasure!

When they reached the swinging stone door, Julian made the slab pivot on its invisible axis, and the Five went through the opening. Julian swung the slab back into place.

So far, everything had gone just as on previous occasions. But suddenly Timmy, leading the way along the tunnel, stopped and gave a low growl, with his nose to the ground.

'What is it, Tim?' asked his mistress.

The clever dog was sniffing suspiciously at something on the floor of the tunnel. George bent down – and picked up a knife! She recognised it at once.

'That's Ivor's knife!' she said. 'The one he was waving about the other day, threatening poor Timmy with it.'

Anne turned quite pale. She realised what the discovery of the knife must mean! Dick said what they were all thinking.

'Our friends the poachers have been here!'

Julian found he was quivering with rage at the thought of those two louts getting into the cave and finding their way to the cavern with the paintings, the crypt, and the secret door. Well, at least they hadn't found out how to open it!

'What luck we shut the door after us!' said George, echoing his thoughts. 'If we'd left it open –'

'Phil and Ivor could have followed us to the valley itself!' said Dick, horrified.

An alarming thought occurred to Anne. 'Perhaps they're not far off at this very minute? Perhaps they're watching out for us?'

'I shouldn't *think* so,' said George. 'They're not to know we're here – and the secret door barred their way to the valley.'

'But even if they've gone home now they're likely to be back tomorrow,' Julian said, frowning. 'We can't risk running into them. George, I think we'd better tell Uncle Quentin about our adventure when we get back this evening. I'm sure Phil and Ivor *have* been following us and spying on us. And they're very close to finding their way to the lost valley too. Even if they did find the way into the underground tunnels and caverns by chance, it comes to much the same thing.'

'I think their motive is pure greed,' said Dick. 'They're probably dreaming of getting their hands on that golden statue – the one in the legend – and they're thinking that even if they can't find it themselves, *we'll* do their work for them and lead them to the treasure.'

'Oh, George, I'm sure Julian is right,' said Anne, who had perfect faith in her elder brother. 'Do let's tell Uncle Quentin *now*! It's the most sensible thing to do.'

But George didn't feel like being sensible. Now that the Five had found out so much, she hated the thought of handing over to some grown-up! It would be so much more satisfying for them to finish the exploration all by themselves.

'Oh, don't let's tell Father just yet!' she begged. 'The moment we do, he'll tell – tell – well, tell whoever you *do* tell in a case like this. Professors and archaeologists and so on, I suppose. And everything will be all stuffy and official, and we won't be allowed to join in the digs or have any chance of finding that statue. We won't be needed here at all any more. I don't know about you, but *I* don't think that's fair!'

Julian and Dick couldn't help agreeing that *they* didn't really think it was fair either. Anne didn't mind about that so much, but she knew she was no good at arguing with her cousin, so in the end

George won everyone round. Julian himself wouldn't have suggested telling Uncle Quentin just yet if he hadn't been worried about Ivor and Phil – he knew just how to carry out a proper archaeological dig, and he had made sure the others were doing it in the right way. And it wasn't that he himself was scared of the two young poachers – just that as the eldest, he felt responsible for the younger children. So he was the hardest for George to persuade.

'Honestly, I'm sure those louts aren't as dangerous as you think, Ju,' she said. 'I mean, they're not clever enough to find out how the stone door swings up – and if we make sure they're not following us, I don't see why we shouldn't finish our explorations! There's something tells me we haven't much farther to go now!'

When Julian did at last give in, he made one condition. 'Now listen, George!' he said. 'I'm still not too happy about this. It would be safer to tell Uncle Quentin – but I can see you're dead against it, so what I suggest is that we give ourselves another twenty-four hours. If we still haven't found the golden statue then, we go to your father. All right?'

George glowered at him – but she really had no choice! Julian was the one she couldn't always boss about.

'Oh, all right,' she said. 'Though I don't suppose we've got much chance of finding the statue in only twenty-four hours! Well – at least we've got the lost valley all to ourselves for another whole day!'

Chapter Ten

THE STATUE

The Five emerged from the underground network of tunnels and caves without meeting Phil and Ivor, in spite of Anne's fears. As the two young poachers themselves had camouflaged the mouth of the cave – as if they thought they were the only ones to have found it – the children thought it was quite possible Ivor and Phil still didn't realise they themselves had been inside.

'Told you so!' said George triumphantly. 'I don't think we need worry about coming back tomorrow.'

The children went an extra long way round Graig village next day, and they looked behind them many times before they risked going anywhere near the entrance to the little cave. Once they were inside, however, Dick wondered out loud whether Phil and Ivor might be inside the caves already.

'I suppose that *is* a possibility,' George admitted. 'So let's try not to make any noise. Timmy will tell us if by any chance they *are* here.'

Timmy was leading the little procession again, and he didn't seem to have got wind of anything suspicious. The Five went through the opening hidden by the swinging door and closed the door again after them. Half an hour later they were busy digging once more.

They ate their picnic on the banks of the river at mid-day, counting up the things they had found that morning: the golden hilt of a knife, a little gold box, three golden discs like those hanging from the necklace Timmy had dug up, and over a dozen stone or earthenware pots and plates.

'But not a sign of any golden statue!' said Dick, sadly.

'All right,' said Julian, a little impatiently, 'there *isn't* much chance that we'll find it today! George said so, and I quite agree.'

Anne didn't say a word. She was looking at George – and George herself was lost in thought and didn't say anything either. But suddenly she jumped to her feet and turned to face her cousins.

'Listen!' said George. 'If that statue of Zulma does exist we needn't expect to find it in any of the houses we've been searching. Zulma was a queen, wasn't she? So she'd live in – well, if not exactly a palace, a rather grander house than anyone else. And *that's* where they'd have put the statue of her after she died – and where we ought to be looking for it now!'

That was all very well! But wherever they looked they couldn't see one of the tower-like houses that looked particularly grand, or any better than the rest.

'If they worshipped the statue as a goddess the Dark Folk might have put it in a sort of alcove somewhere,' Anne ventured to suggest. 'Would it be possible –'

But she was interrupted by George, who let out a yell of delight.

'Good thinking *again*, Anne!' she cried. 'The waterfall! The rock wall behind it is full of hollows and holes worn away by the force of the water. I noticed when we were going along the ledge. The hollows are just like alcoves. One of them might have the statue in it, well camouflaged!'

She was already chasing back to the great water-fall, with her cousins hot on her heels.

And George and Anne were right! In the very middle of the cliff behind the waterfall, some moss-grown stones hid a kind of alcove. Once they had moved the stones away, the children found them-selves facing a golden statue about the height of a child of ten.

'Oh, isn't she lovely!' cried Anne.

She was right. The statue's face was that of an extraordinarily beautiful woman. The waterfall cast quivering greenish light on its sweetly smiling features.

'Yes, she *is* lovely,' said George. 'You're right,

Anne. But look at the size of her! She's going to be difficult to move. A solid gold statue that big must weigh an awful lot.'

'If we leave her here, we risk Ivor and Phil finding her before Uncle Quentin can get in touch with the authorities, though,' Dick pointed out.

Julian, who was standing on the narrow ledge beside the statue, put out his hands as if to pick it up.

'Watch out, Ju!' his brother warned him. 'She'll be too heavy for you – and if she knocks you off balance –'

But he never finished his sentence! Queen Zulma was moving in Julian's hands – and Julian had *not* been knocked off balance.

'Come on, help me!' he told the others. 'She's heavy all right, but not *too* heavy. I think the four of us can get her out of here between us.'

Sure enough, the statue weighed less than you might have thought, looking at it. The children managed to get it out of its alcove and over to the right-hand bank, where they put it down.

'That's amazing!' said Dick, a little breathlessly. 'A solid statue that size ought to weigh a lot more.'

'Well, anyone can see why!' said George. 'The legend's wrong about the statue being solid! It must be hollow instead.'

'Hollow?' asked Anne, puzzled.

'Well, yes, of course – or we'd never have been able to move it. And if it *is* hollow – my goodness, it might have something important inside!'

'Another treasure!' cried Anne.

'I wonder?' murmured Julian. 'A statue acting as a kind of strong-box?'

'Let's see if we can find any way to look inside it!' said George.

They carefully laid the statue flat on the ground – and discovered its secret at once! There was a plinth at its base, closed with a kind of stopper which the children worked gently out. Inside, they saw a cavity.

'So I was right!' said George.

Her cousins held their breath as she put her hand inside the hollow statue, and brought out a sealed cylinder made of some lightweight metal. When George shook it, they could all hear something rattling inside!

It was not very easy to open the cylinder, but Julian did it, taking great care not to damage anything. It came apart at last – and out fell some scrolls of rolled-up parchment covered in tiny writing.

'I *say*!' breathed Julian. 'Manuscripts!'

'They're in a foreign language,' said Dick, rather disappointed. 'And in a kind of alphabet we can't read, too!'

'I bet they're about the history of the Dark Folk!' said George eagerly. 'My word – these must be even *more* precious and interesting than the gold!'

'Better put them back in their case and put that back in the statue,' Dick suggested.

'Yes, you're right,' agreed Julian. 'Then they

won't come to any harm. After that we'll wrap Queen Zulma in our plastic macs, and if we're very careful and we all lend a hand, I think we can get her safely back to Magga Glen farmhouse. Then we'll hand her over to Uncle Quentin, and that will be the end of our adventure.'

'A jolly good adventure it was, too!' said Dick cheerfully. And he seized hold of Timmy's front paws and made him dance round in a circle! Even Julian, who was usually so reserved, joined in the victory dance – and George took Anne's hand and danced around the statue with her. They were all shouting and singing for joy, and Timmy added his own excited barking to the din.

And then, suddenly, everyone fell silent. The shouting and dancing stopped dead, and the Five clustered around Queen Zulma in alarm, hardly daring to breathe.

They had been counting their chickens before they were hatched! As if by magic, those unpleasant louts Ivor and Phil had materialised before their very eyes. And they were not alone! There were two other tall and dangerous-looking youths with them.

'Hallo, kids!' said Phil, laughing in a nasty way. 'Didn't expect to see us, did you? No, indeed! Thought you could get away from us, eh? Well then, it's wrong you were! We've had our eye on *you* – with a little bit of help from Evan and Rhys here, and binoculars now and then! That swinging door gave us a bit of trouble, but we solved the problem, didn't we, now?'

As they were there in the valley, it was only too clear that they *had* solved the problem!

Ivor added, with a sly smile, 'And Evan and Rhys will help us with the statue there – the one you've so kindly found for us! Would there be any more treasures to find in here, I wonder?'

His greedy eyes were roaming over the whole of the lost valley – the waterfall, the river and the round, tower-like houses.

Four tough young men facing four brave children: it was a strange sight! And the statue of Queen Zulma seemed to be smiling enigmatically at it in the greenish light that fell from the roof of the enormous cave.

George was simply disgusted to think of all the trouble she and her cousins had been to, only to be outwitted in the end! She couldn't say a word. And a word was all Timmy was waiting for to fling himself on the poachers – but she knew it wouldn't have been safe for him. Julian and Dick were rooted to the spot with surprise and anger, just like their cousin George.

But little Anne, the youngest of all and usually the most timid, suddenly forgot to be frightened of the louts! She was boiling with rage, and she had to let it out somehow. She always *did* turn out to be brave when it really mattered, and this time was no exception. Raising her sweet little voice as high as she could, she stood there and told the four young men off.

'You ought to be ashamed of yourselves!' she cried. 'Fancy being cowardly enough to attack children! And you've got no right to this statue! *We* found it – and we're not keeping it for ourselves either! My uncle will hand it over to the sort of experts who'll know what to do with it, and if you take it away from us by force you'll – you'll just be horrible *thieves*!'

Phil roared with laughter.

'You don't say!' he said. 'Hear the little girl, did you all? Who does she think she is? Come along – let's grab the statue and get away, and if these kids accuse us of anything later we just deny it! I'd like to know what they think they can do about *that*!'

Julian had instinctively placed himself in front of the statue as if to protect it. George was furious – and she reacted furiously! This was no time for cool thought! She flung herself on Ivor, who was closest to her – and dear old Timmy sprang to her aid unasked.

Dick was stung into action too – he made a dive for the youth called Evan and got hold of his ankles. Anne's courage had given out, and she was yelling with alarm as Rhys advanced towards her with one hand raised.

It was a pitched battle – but not a fair one. What could four children do against four tall, strong young men who were determined to lay their hands on a treasure – even if the children had a dog to help them? It was all too obvious how the fight would finish. Dick brought Evan to the ground, but he was soon on his feet again, and as he was twice Dick's size he soon overpowered the boy and tied his hands with a piece of rope. Phil had made straight for Julian, who was clinging to the statue, and snatched it away from him. Rhys didn't even have to hit Anne to make her stop screaming – she realised very quickly that it was no use resisting, and let him tie her hands together.

That left George, Timmy and Ivor. George was really laying into the poacher, fists and feet flying, and she had splendid support from Timmy, whose teeth were sunk firmly into the seat of his enemy's trousers!

Ivor did not like this undignified position a bit! He decided not to wait for his friends to come to his aid – instead, he put his hand in his pocket and brought out an aerosol spray containing tear gas. He sprayed the gas straight in George's face – her eyes began to water painfully at once. Blinded by the gas, she raised her hands to her face, and to do that she had to let go of Ivor. Ivor swung round to Timmy, and dealt with the dog in the same way. Poor Timmy! He let out a pitiful yowl and started whirling round and round on the spot. He couldn't see anything, and the gas made him sneeze. He couldn't even *smell* anything, and usually he relied on his wonderful nose to tell him where his enemies were.

But only a few yards away, another fight was still going on . . .

Anne and Dick might be helpless, with their

hands tied, and George and Timmy were unable to do anything for the time being, but Julian had kept his head. He was tall and strong for his age – and forgetting that his opponents outnumbered him, he flung himself on Phil as the young man attacked him, giving as good as he got. He struck out hard with both fists.

The young poacher hadn't been expecting such tough opposition. He was taken by surprise, slipped, and lost his balance. Jumping up again, however, he lunged at Julian. Julian, who was standing with his back to the river, ducked aside. And that was just too bad for Phil! Carried away by the force of his own blow, he lost his balance once again – and this time he plunged head-first straight into the foaming waters of the river.

It all happened so quickly that the others, watching, simply stood there open-mouthed for several seconds on end. Only Phil's despairing cries brought them back to reality.

'Help!' he shouted. 'Help! I'm drowning!'

Chapter Eleven

THE END OF A WONDERFUL ADVENTURE

The young poacher went down once and then came up to the surface of the water again. He was struggling frantically in his efforts to reach the bank. Everyone could see that he wasn't going to make it, and he was in real danger.

'The current's too strong – it's carrying him away!' said Dick, horrified.

Ivor wasn't striking any fine attitudes now – he was trembling all over.

'Phil – Phil!' he cried. 'He's done for – he can't swim much. Oh no! And if we go to help him *we'll* be swept away too!'

Julian looked desperately around him. If only he could see a piece of wood long enough for him to hold it out to Phil! But there was very little wood of any sort in the valley. Meanwhile, Phil had given up shouting as the river carried him away – all his strength went into his efforts to fight its torrential waters.

Anne had gone white as a sheet. She put her bound hands to her eyes, so as not to have to watch this dreadful scene. Rhys and Evan, struck almost dumb with horror, could do nothing but mutter, 'He's drowning!' As if *that* did any good!

'Oh, look!' Dick suddenly cried. 'He's caught hold of something!'

The current had carried Phil over to the opposite bank, and making one last great effort he had managed to grab a rock that stuck up just above the surface of the water. But the current was still tearing at his body, trying to sweep him away, and he was in danger of losing his grip.

'He won't be able to hold on long!' said Dick, shuddering.

Julian had already got his scout knife out of his pocket and was cutting his brother's bonds. 'Quick — let's go round by way of the waterfall and help him!' he said breathlessly, and turning to the three appalled young men, he added, 'You follow me too! You can help me haul your friend out of the water.'

In his heart, Julian knew they didn't stand much chance of success. It was going to take a little while for all of them to get past the waterfall in single file and run down the bank to the spot where Phil was clinging to his rock. The odds were about a thousand to one that he would have had to let go before they reached him — he seemed to have very little strength left in him now. But Julian knew, too, that they had to try.

While Julian and Dick (who knew what they were doing) and Ivor, Evan and Rhys (who didn't) were making for the waterfall, Anne stayed where she was, sobbing. She could tell that Phil's life was hanging by a thread.

Suddenly, the little girl found that instead she was watching a most unexpected sight.

She had thought George and Timmy were as helpless as she was – but they arrived on the scene as if by magic!

Hearing Phil's cries for help, George had made a desperate effort to get her eyes open. The tears flowing down her cheeks showed how much her eyelids were still stinging. But though her vision was blurred, she could see what danger the young poacher was in. She took the situation in at once. Phil was the worst of their enemies – but George immediately forgot about that as she wondered how she could save his life.

'Timmy!' she called. 'Come on, old boy!'

And she made for the river, quite sure her faithful dog would follow her, even though he was still whimpering with pain.

She was going to try something extremely rash – but she didn't think of that at the time. It simply didn't occur to her that she was risking her own life to go to the young man's aid.

She was a very good swimmer, and she kept herself in training – at home in Kirrin she spent as much time as she could in the water. But this was a different sort of water: an immensely strong current sweeping on towards a wide crevice, through which the river disappeared into what, so far as any of them knew, was a bottomless ravine.

Never mind! The brave little girl didn't hesitate for a moment. She waited only to take her shoes off and then plunged boldly into the water. Timmy jumped straight in after her.

Anne uttered a cry of terror. Hearing it, Julian, Dick and the others turned round.

'George!' cried the two boys both at once. 'Come back, George!'

But George didn't even hear them. She was swimming for all she was worth, fighting against the current. When she reached the middle of the river she was afraid it would sweep her away, on past Phil. She made a great effort and swam on. Every now and then she was caught in a wild eddy of water and disappeared from sight, only to emerge a little farther on, gradually making her way across the river. Timmy followed her, and never took his eyes off his little mistress.

At long last she came level with Phil. He was at the end of his tether, and was obviously about to let go. He looked at her, wild-eyed, unable to grasp what she was doing.

'It's all right – just hold on!' George told him.

She clung to the same rock and supported him with her free hand. That would mean he could hang on a little longer. But now she was in great danger herself.

Timmy was quite close to her. He could keep

himself afloat easily enough, but he didn't seem to be able to do anything to help her, and his own strength would soon give out.

'Oh, I wish to goodness I hadn't dragged *him* into this,' thought George. 'Poor old Timmy – if *he* drowns –'

But then she had a pleasant surprise. Not only was Timmy holding his own against the current, the good, intelligent dog suddenly showed his powers of initiative. He took Phil's trousers in his mouth, level with the belt at the waistband, and started pulling against the current. This was a great help – the force of the current against the poacher's body was less, and it was not pulling so hard at his and George's arms.

George felt a great sense of relief. 'But whatever we do we mustn't let go!' she thought, and she said, out loud, 'That's right, Phil, just hold on tight!'

And at long, long last Julian and the others came running up. They flung themselves flat on the bank, quite out of breath, and between them all they managed to haul George and Phil out of the water.

It could have been a disaster, but it ended on a comic note! When Phil came up on the bank he was followed by good old Timmy, still with his teeth sunk into the young man's trousers! He had probably realised that this was the best way to make sure he was fished out himself – not that anyone would have forgotten *him*.

After all the suspense of the last few minutes,

everyone was relieved and delighted by the success of the tricky rescue operation. Julian and Dick couldn't stop hugging George and Timmy. Ivor, Evan and Rhys were slapping Phil on the back – Phil himself was choking, still feeling more or less suffocated. They were all talking at once.

'George, that was a crazy thing to do!'

'You're a heroine straight out of a story book, though!'

'You okay, Phil? That was a fright you gave us, indeed!'

'Woof! Woof!'

Over on the opposite bank, Anne had managed to wriggle her hands free and was clapping them happily, jumping up and down for joy. Phil managed to pull himself together. He went over to George.

'Thanks,' he said gruffly. 'Well – thanks! That was really good of you! I'd have been done for, but for you and your dog!' And he added, even more embarrassed than before, 'I – er, I'd like to say sorry! You're a really good fellow!'

What with all the drama and confusion, he had quite forgotten that George was really a girl!

She smiled, and shook hands. 'That's all right!' she said. 'Let's be friends! And to prove we *are* friends, you can all help us get that statue to safety!'

Ivor and the others were impressed by George's generosity, and they all followed the example of their leader Phil.

'We'd better hurry up,' said Julian, making his agile way back past the waterfall again. 'George and Phil are both soaked. They need to get dry as soon as possible.'

Anne was delighted to see everyone back safe and sound. With the help of the four young men, the children easily got the statue out through the caves and tunnels into the open air. It was still wrapped in a rather undignified way in their plastic macs.

Rhys had a little car, and he took George, Timmy and Julian on board, along with the statue, promising to drive them down to Magga Glen in record time. After that he came back again for Dick, Anne and the bicycles. As for Phil, Ivor and Evan, they made their own way home.

The drive to Magga Glen wasn't far. Rhys dropped the first party and drove straight off again. Julian and George watched him leave in a great hurry, and burst out laughing.

'He obviously didn't want to face Uncle Quentin!' said Julian.

'I'm not so sure that *I* do, either!' said George ruefully. 'I'm wet through – and the adventure might not have ended so well! You know how strict my father can be! Oh, well . . .'

'You'd better go and change straight away,' Julian advised her. 'And then we'll wait for Dick and Anne to arrive, and take the statue into the living room and unwrap it – and we'll tell Aunt Fanny first! How about that? Then *she* can break the news to Uncle Quentin!'

That was a good idea of Julian's. And anyway, just for once, Uncle Quentin was so fascinated by the golden statue and the documents it contained, not to mention the other amazing discoveries the children had made, that he quite forgot to tell them off for their rashness!

'This business will make quite a stir!' he said. 'As for you children, I imagine you're likely to find yourselves in the headlines again.'

He was right, too. George, Julian, Dick and Anne found themselves the centre of attention over the next few days. Quite soon, a whole crowd of scholars and archaeologists descended on the quiet little Welsh village to investigate the lost valley, and the settlement of Temulka. They dug up more treasures to add to those the children had already found. Meanwhile, another team of learned men and women were busy deciphering the documents that had been hidden inside the statue.

And one fine day, feeling very proud and happy, George and her cousins were invited to attend an official meeting at which the secret history of the Dark Folk of Mount Graig was to be revealed – the history they had left behind them in those precious documents.

It was a great day for George. Dogs don't usually go to important scientific or historical meetings, but Timmy was given special permission to go with her. And all the mysteries were explained at last.

After the meeting, which had been really exciting, the Five went back to Magga Glen farmhouse for an extra-special tea. Mrs Jones had been hard at work, baking delicious home-made bread and Welsh cakes, and there were raspberries and cream, and iced shortbread biscuits.

They had tea out of doors in the garden, still talking about all they had heard.

'So the Dark Folk *did* live in Temulka, and they once really had a queen called Zulma – or if she wasn't exactly a queen, she was their honoured leader!' said George.

'And of course they didn't actually make gold,' said Julian, 'but just as I thought, they'd found a huge vein of gold ore in Mount Graig.'

'And apparently the hunters' dogs were specially trained not to bark, so as not to give their masters away!' added George. 'I bet *you* were interested in that bit, Timmy!'

Anne liked the more romantic bits of the story. She summed them up, her eyes shining. 'The people of Temulka were wise and prudent, and if they ever left their valley home they did so as inconspicuously as they could – just to go hunting or pick medicinal herbs on the mountainside. Zulma dried the herbs, and used them to cure sicknesses – she was a great healer!'

'I'm not so sure I believe the bit in one of the documents that said she'd invented an elixir that made you live longer,' said Dick, being rather more down-to-earth than his sister.

Julian didn't want anything like a quarrel, so he hastily changed the subject. 'And the Dark Folk *were* musical!'

'They were good artists, too, judging by those cave paintings,' said George. 'Think of so much talent being drowned by the river!'

And for a moment the children sat thinking sadly of those long-ago people. They felt as if they actually knew them quite well, by now, and they hated to think of the water sweeping them away.

Then they came back to the present!

'There's going to be a museum opened in Graig village,' said Julian. 'I expect it will attract a lot of tourists!'

'That will do this part of Wales good, I'm sure,' said Anne. 'Mrs Jones will never be short of guests wanting to rent her rooms – but I hope she won't have so many that she can't have us to stay again too!'

'It's nice to think we've found out a little bit of ancient history that nobody knew before,' said Dick.

'Woof!' agreed Timmy – as if he knew anything about ancient history!

But George had the last word.

'If you ask me,' she said, 'the best part of the whole adventure was making friends with Phil and Co. in the end! I don't think they'll ever go poaching or stealing things again. And that's worth all the gold statues in the world!'

NICHOLAS FISK

THE STARSTORMER SAGA

STARSTORMERS
SUNBURST
CATFANG
EVIL EYE
VOLCANO

The four Starstormers are Vawn, Ispex, Tsu and Makenzi. They construct a spaceship from pieces of scrap and, together with their robot Shambles, take off into deepest space. *Starstormer* takes them into a thrilling series of space adventures, including strange encounters on alien planets and a continual and dangerous battle against the wicked Octopus Emperor.

KNIGHT BOOKS

If you've enjoyed this book, you may like to read some of the Knight titles listed on the following pages:

A Royal Mail service in association with the Book Marketing Council & The Booksellers Association.

Post-A-Book is a Post Office trademark.

ENID BLYTON

A COMPLETE LIST OF THE FAMOUS FIVE ADVENTURES

KNIGHT BOOKS

WILLARD PRICE

A COMPLETE LIST OF HIS THRILLING ANIMAL ADVENTURES

KNIGHT BOOKS